HAGBA

HAGBANE'S DOOM

John Houghton

KINGSWAY PUBLICATIONS

EASTBOURNE

First published 1984
Reprinted 1984
Reprinted 1985

ISBN 0 86065 287 4

Front cover design by Vic Mitchell

Printed in Great Britain for
KINGSWAY PUBLICATIONS LTD
Lottbridge Drove, Eastbourne, E. Sussex BN23 6NT.
Typeset by Nuprint Services Ltd, Harpenden, Herts.
Printed and bound in Great Britain
by Collins, Glasgow

To Deborah, Sharon and Stephen
and the pupils of Baring Primary School
whose enthusiasm helped create this story

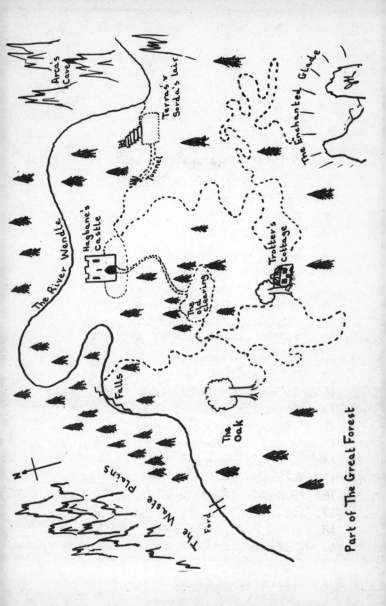

Part of The Great Forest

Contents

Prologue

A solitary flame burned bright in the emptiness of night. It seemed to beckon Oswain and he drifted towards its glow as though in a trance. The flame grew higher and higher until it filled the sea of dreams upon which he floated. As he looked, he thought he could see faces flickering to life in the fire which burned before him. A freckle-faced boy, followed by a girl with deep, dark eyes, and then a smiling lad, each so alive, so real that he might have spoken to them had they not dissolved again into the flame. Oswain wondered who they might be.

A silent wind blew upon the blaze so that it flickered in a confusion of light. Another image began to form and his heart beat in wild panic, for never had he seen a face so evil. For a brief eternity it hovered before him, red-rimmed eyes glaring so hatefully that he would have turned and fled if he could. But our dreams do not let us run away, and so he watched with horror until the face crumbled to ashes and only the flame burned on.

The tongue of fire parted down the centre to reveal an endless, lonely blackness. Then he spied a single dot of light in the far distance. The light grew in size, rushing towards him at incalculable speed, until it filled the screen of his mind with dazzling brightness, and he recognized the glory of the splendid jewel which hung before his eyes.

'The Merestone,' whispered Oswain, who then awoke abruptly to find himself lying on the floor of his chamber. Slowly, and slightly shaking, he arose and made his way to the window where he gazed out across the sleeping city over which his father ruled. All was quiet. Then, almost without his being aware of it, his eye was lifted to the night sky. There, hanging like a pearl in the velvet blackness, one star glittered more brightly than the rest. He glanced at the ring on his second finger. The silver sliver of stone it contained glinted in response.

'My destiny calls me. Elmesh has spoken.' He uttered the words quietly but firmly to himself and then turned to prepare for the journey which he knew lay ahead.

.   .   *   .   .

High in that same night sky, though many miles distant, in the stark emptiness of snow-crested mountains, a mighty white eagle felt a light tug in the wind. It was nothing more, but Arca, whose senses were tuned to a fine degree, knew that he had received a command. His time had also come, and from that moment he flew steadily south.

The adventure had begun.

Chapter One

THE OLD OAK

'Hoi, mind my head, Peter. Ouch!'

'I can't help it, this ladder is so old and wobbly. I'm doing my best. Sorry anyway.'

'Oh, stop moaning you two and get on with it,' said Andrew from further down the ladder. 'Anyway, I don't know what you're complaining about, Sarah, 'cos if it breaks, I get you both on top of me!'

'Well, it'll give us a soft landing then,' called Peter. 'Perhaps we should try it and see.'

'Just you dare!'

The three Brown children were climbing a massive oak tree at the far end of Uncle Joe's orchard. It was the Spring Bank Holiday and they had come down to stay for a week at his cottage just outside Abbotsbury in Dorset. The day after they arrived, their parents had taken them around the swannery and the sub-tropical gardens. It had been good fun but they were delighted today to be given an opportunity to explore by themselves.

Uncle Joe owned quite a few acres of land including a large garden, a vegetable plot and an old orchard. The orchard was furthest from the cottage and the children had wandered to the far end. Various woodland trees grew there, but what had caught their attention at once was the old oak. It was the sort of tree which invited you to scale its branches. A brief search had produced a rickety old ladder which would get them to the lowest boughs and, after a brief debate as to who should go first (which ended as it nearly always did), they began to climb in age order.

Peter was fourteen and freckled. He wore a checked shirt and jeans and an untidy mop of brown hair. Like his father, he was good-natured and easy going.

His younger sister Sarah was a thoughtful twelve-year-old who enjoyed walking alone and watching waves beat on the sea-shore. Today she wore her favourite red blouse and a pair of old dungarees. And she had asked her mother to put her blonde hair into plaits.

Eleven-year-old Andrew made up the terrible trio, as their father affectionately called them. He was wearing old corduroys and a green shirt and, as always, an enthusiastic grin.

You will have realized that these were the faces which Oswain had seen in his dream.

'Wow, there's a smashing fork in the tree here. Come on, you two. Hey, we could build a tree house here, then we could pretend we were being attacked by natives and wild animals. And we'd have to live off emergency rations.'

'And then Mum will call us in for tea,' puffed Sarah as she scrambled up to join him.

'Gosh, what a view,' gasped Andrew. 'You can see right over the apple trees from here. It's fantastic! We must be twenty feet up at least. What do you think, Sarah?'

Before his sister could answer, Peter called them

over to the other side of the great fork in the tree.

'Hey, you two, come and have a look at this. Look, there's a massive hole leading into the tree. It must be hollow.'

'Why, it's big enough to get into, if you crouch,' said Sarah. 'Do you think we should try?'

'There's probably a gorilla or a snake hiding in there. Creep inside and it'll grab you by the throat....' Andrew tried to imitate what it was like to be strangled by a gorilla twenty feet up in a tree. The others looked at him pityingly.

Peter peered into the gloomy hole. 'It's very dark but my eyes are getting used to it. It seems to go in for about a metre and then it drops down. I'm going to have a look.'

So saying, he crept inside. 'Hey, this is odd, there are steps leading down into the tree,' he exclaimed. 'Come and see.'

The three of them crowded in and stared in amazement. There, sure enough, was a flight of stairs descending steeply into the tree trunk.

'Mighty clever gorilla, that's all I can say,' said Peter.

'How on earth did they get there?'

'Where do they go?'

'We must explore now. This is fantastic!'

'Yes, let's see how far down they go,' suggested Peter.

'I don't know. I'm not sure I want to. Don't you think we should tell Mum first and....' But Sarah never finished her sentence as the boys gave her withering looks. 'Oh, all right, I'm coming,' she said.

And so, with this simple decision, the three children began their strange descent into the warm brownness of the great tree.

It was at the seventh step down that they felt it—a puff of air and a kind of shiver. Later, when they tried, they could not really describe it, except that they felt tingly and goosebumpy all over. But something had happened, some barrier had been passed which committed them to going ever deeper into the darkness and whatever awaited them.

'It must go right to the bottom of the tree at this rate,' muttered Peter.

'More like the bottom of the world,' Sarah replied. She was wondering if they would ever get out again.

'Hey, I can see daylight. It must come out at ground level.'

'That's odd though, 'cos I've counted fifty steps so far,' exclaimed Andrew.

'Hmm, still here we are back in the gar...' Peter stared and shivered. Suddenly he felt a bit sick.

'What is it, Pete? What's the matter? Oh! Oh dear.'

'It's not our garden!'

They stared blankly at the scene which confronted them. Instead of a pleasant spring orchard they were surrounded by a vast forest of ancient trees. And all the branches were bare, as in winter. Many of them lay broken like twisted serpents of stone on the ground. The smell of decay hung in the dank air. All was silent and lifeless, still as death. Not a bird sang.

'Wh-where are we?' stuttered Sarah. 'It's like some kind of petrified forest. I don't like it at all and I feel frightened. Honest I do. Can we go back? I said we shouldn't have come.'

'Oh, shush a moment will you?' said Peter. 'Something very odd has happened to us and I want to know what it is. I've a feeling we can't go back—at least, not yet anyway.'

'The seventh step down it was,' Andrew added. 'I felt all kind of funny inside. I agree with Peter. We're here and somehow we're meant to be. So we'd better find out what it's all about. I'm all for exploring.'

By now Sarah had ceased shaking and a light had come into her dark eyes. 'Yes, I got the feeling too. I'm sorry, it's silly to be afraid. So lead on, big brother.' She smiled at Peter. 'But let's go carefully for all that.'

They tied one of Sarah's red ribbons to the oak to help them find it again and began to walk cautiously through the trees.

'There's hardly any sign of life anywhere,' observed Peter. 'This forest is almost dead. Just a bit of moss and a few bushes growing. I wonder what happened to it?'

'Hmm, it's not dead but, well, as though someone has taken all the life out of it.'

'Well, silly, it must be dead then,' laughed Andrew, breaking their seriousness.

'No, that's not what I mean. What I'm trying to say is. . . .'

But before Sarah could venture on her explanation there was a rustling and a crashing from the dead undergrowth around them and, in a twinkling of an eye, they were surrounded by fierce-looking animals armed with spears and clubs.

'One move and you die! Stay right where you are.'

The speaker was an important-looking stoat. But the children could not have moved even if they had tried. It's bad enough to find yourself where you did not, even in your wildest dreams, expect to be. But to be confronted by animals which speak and then to realize that something has happened to your size and theirs, or both, so that you are more or less the same size but trees still look right, well, that is all too much.

The ring of animals closed in—rabbits, foxes, weasels, moles, squirrels. Fierce eyes and bared teeth made it quite clear that they were far from friendly. And the prods and pricks which the children received were real enough to prove this was no dream.

'Tie them up and take them away,' the stoat commanded.

At once the animals swarmed over them, pushing all three to the ground. Sarah started to scream but a gag was promptly tied tightly across her mouth. Rough ropes bound their hands behind their backs in spite of their frantic struggles. It seemed only a matter of seconds before they were quite helpless. Then, as quickly as they had been smothered by the furry creatures, they were dragged to their feet and, encouraged by the spears, were marched along a twisting narrow pathway through the undergrowth.

As they stumbled along Peter began to pull himself together. Clearly they had landed into some strange adventure by a magic staircase and had immediately been caught by hostile creatures. They must escape somehow. But that was obviously not possible at the moment. He tried to keep track of the twists and turns but soon realized that he had no idea of the way back.

He noticed that the pace was getting faster and many of the animals were glancing nervously over their shoulders as though expecting to be chased. Perhaps there was someone who would come to their rescue, Peter thought, and this gave him comfort. In fact the company was almost running by the time they reached the end of the trail and came to a panting halt in a small clearing. The children waited in trepidation, trying to get their breath through the smelly gags. If only they could ask some questions!

The stoat, who was obviously in command, nodded to their closest captors and the three children were pushed forwards towards a tall, imposing elm tree. At first they could not see why. Then they noticed a dark hole near the roots. Sarah wondered if this led upstairs to home or downstairs to somewhere else. Andrew thought it might be a prison. Prods from behind soon had all three crowded reluctantly in the entrance, staring into the gloom.

It was Peter who saw them first, a pair of slant yellow eyes glowing out of the darkness and moving towards them! Panic welled up and their minds filled with nameless dreads. They turned wildly but were squarely met by a mass of sharp-pointed spears. There was no escape, and slowly the children were driven helplessly backwards into the black hole to meet the unknown horror which glared at them.

Chapter Two

MR AND MRS TROTTER

'What do you want done with 'em, Aldred, sir?'

The eyes spoke and materialized into the form of a fox.

'Are they spies? More of *her* work, eh!'

'That's right, Foxy,' the stoat replied. 'Caught them up by the old oak. Strange looking creatures, aren't they? Not like her usual work and not very strong either. We overpowered them just like that.'

'What weapons did they have, sir?'

'That's the odd thing, they've got none. Unless it's some secret magic we don't know about. That's why I want Trotter to see them.'

'Very good, sir. I'll fetch him.'

The children were pushed through a door at the end of the short dark tunnel and found themselves standing in a small bare room which was lit from a window high up on one wall. Relief flooded through them as they realized that Foxy was no more than a guard and not some terrible monster about to devour them. The room appeared to be quite civilized and they hoped that this Trotter would allow them to explain who they were. They had not long to wait, for another door opened and in walked a venerable old badger.

Aldred stepped forward smartly and saluted. All the other animals had remained outside with the exception of a hedgehog who continued to menace them with his fearsome looking bristles.

'Strange spies, Trotter, sir. We caught them by the old oak. Truth is, sir, I don't know quite what to make of them, so I brought them to you as soon as possible. What do you think she's up to this time?'

The badger stepped forward and peered at the children through wire-rimmed spectacles. Sarah thought he had kindly eyes. For about a minute he looked them over, saying not a word. Then he spoke quietly.

'Loose their bonds and remove those gags.'

This task was quickly performed and with great sighs of relief the children rubbed their sore wrists and stretched their aching muscles. Peter was just about to blurt out a mixture of questions and explanations when the badger held up a paw. Then, to the amazement of everyone in the room, he slowly went down on to one knee before them.

'Children of men, for that is who you are, is it not?' he asked gravely. 'My name is Trotter and I bid you welcome to the Great Forest. You have come as it is written. Elmesh be praised! Would you please forgive us for the rude welcome which we gave you, but these are perilous days, and we did not know the hour of your coming. Nor would it have been wise for us to know, lest *she* were to discover it. My guards were but doing their duty.'

Before anybody else could speak, Aldred blurted out, 'But are you sure, sir? Are you saying these are on our side? That Elmesh has sent them?'

'Of course. Did I not tell you that I had received indications of their coming and of what to look for?' He

18

rose and turned to Peter. 'It *is* true that you are the children of men?'

Peter found himself stammering. 'W-w-well, y-yes, I suppose so. Only we aren't usually called that. I say, look, what is all this? Where are we? How is it you can speak? I don't understand what's happened to us. Is it some kind of dream?'

Trotter rumbled a laugh deep in his throat. 'Too many questions at once. And I thought you were coming with answers! Never mind, never mind, Elmesh has strange ways. I will answer your questions as best I am able. But first, I understand, a cup of tea would be in order. You must come and meet Mrs Trotter. She will be most interested.'

There was a kindly authority in the badger's voice and Sarah warmed to him at once. 'A cup of tea would be marvellous,' she said, 'and we'd love to meet Mrs Trotter.'

With great politeness the badger ushered them through the door by which he had entered and they found themselves in a delightful cottage room. Gleaming brasses and glowing copper complemented wooden beams and soft armchairs. A small log fire burned in the smoke-blackened fireplace and flowery curtains decorated leaded windows. Obviously they had entered by a kind of back door into the badger's home.

'What a pretty house!' exclaimed Sarah. 'It's beautiful!'

'I'm glad you like it, my dear.' Mrs Trotter bustled in, wearing a frilly apron. 'You're very welcome to our house. That is, if you're not friends of *her*.'

'My dear, may I introduce you to the children of men. They have come, as I said.'

'Oh well, pleased to meet you, I'm sure, but is that the only name you have?' she enquired.

The children took to her at once and Andrew replied cheerily, 'It's nice to meet you Mrs T. I'm Andrew and she's Sarah and that's Peter.'

Mrs Trotter laughed. 'Why, that's better. You are so serious sometimes, dear,' she scolded her husband gently. 'Well, I expect you would like a nice cup of tea,' she said to the children. 'Make yourselves at home. Sit down, my dears.'

She hurried back to the kitchen as they flopped into the armchairs. 'I like your wife, Mr Trotter,' said Peter, laughing, 'but please answer some of our questions.'

'Yes, of course,' replied the badger settling himself into an old sofa by the fireside. 'So, you do not know where you are or why you are here? That is strange but perhaps hardly surprising as the utmost secrecy will have been kept by Elmesh. But that is very secret: not even to tell the deliverers who they are!' He smiled to himself.

'Um, excuse me, but who is El.. Elmesh?' interrupted Sarah.

'Elmesh, who is Elmesh?' exclaimed Trotter. 'You don't know? Elmesh just is. Without him there would be nothing, nothing at all. Why, the whole Great Forest is because Elmesh is. And the sun and stars. It is he who has sent you just as it was written long ago.'

'But all we did was climb a tree and go down some steps inside,' said Andrew. 'I just don't get it.'

'Ah, that tree! That oak has something special about it. It is a kind of doorway, but only at certain times, I am told. This is one of Elmesh's times. Things are about to happen, if I am not very much mistaken.'

'You said we were to be deliverers?' enquired Peter. 'What did you mean?'

Trotter's answer was delayed by the entry of Mrs Trotter laden with tea and cakes. For a few minutes nothing was said as hungry mouths devoured the mouthwatering goodies before them. Then Trotter said he would try to begin at the beginning.

'Long years ago, before our present troubles began, the Great Forest was beautiful and fair to look upon. Birds sang in every tree and scented shrubs bloomed everywhere. The forest-folk roamed free and food was abundant. I remember those days of long ago, when I was young,' he mused. 'What great times we had. Not a care in the world. Oh, we all knew Elmesh looked after things and we used to visit the enchanted glade sometimes to gaze upon the Merestone. The elders taught us that this was the secret of the Forest's beauty and certainly to be near it was a wonderful experience. Why, if you hurt yourself, just to go there made you better. And those who would be wise spent long hours gazing at it and learning the ways of Elmesh.'

'Did you do that?' asked Sarah eagerly.

'Yes I did, but long ago now, for, alas, all that has changed. A great tragedy has come upon us. *She* came one fateful day and stole the Merestone.' His face filled with sorrow as he spoke. 'Then she returned to enslave the Great Forest. Our happy days came to an end. The Forest began to wither and die all around us; flowers ceased blooming and the birds fled. Food has become scarce and the forest-folk live in fear of their lives. That is why we have to defend ourselves,' he explained.

'But who is *she*?' queried Peter.

'Hagbane!' Aldred, who had been listening, spat the word out. 'Hagbane the witch. She stole the

Merestone and brought this evil upon us. She dominates us all from her castle and nobody can touch her whilst she holds it. We are almost helpless.' His shoulders sagged and the children felt pity for a soldier bravely fighting on knowing he was defeated.

'Well, I'm not afraid of any silly witch. We'll just go and kick her door in and get your Merestone back!' declared Andrew stoutly.

'Alas, I do not think it will be quite that simple,' Trotter replied. 'Yes, I do believe you will help deliver us from Hagbane's power, for it is written that it should be so, but you will find that she is no light foe to tackle. Many of our folk have tried and now languish in her dungeons, or worse.'

'Where do we fit into all this?' enquired Peter. 'Because we seem to be the most unlikely witch fighters I can think of.'

In answer to his question the badger ushered them into a library filled with dusty brown books and parchments.

'I have studied the ways of Elmesh for long years. Many hours I have sat in the enchanted glade and gazed into the pool. I have looked upon the light of the star El-la, Elmesh's star, as it reflected in the water. And to me was entrusted the ancient scrolls of the Great Forest so that I am recognized as the lore-master amongst the forest-folk. Five nights ago I had a vision in my sleep in which I saw your faces by the light of El-la. I knew the time was at hand and I read the prophecy again.'

'Can we see what it says?' chorused the children.

'It is written in an ancient script but I will translate it roughly for you.' He took up an old yellowed parchment covered in strange symbols and began to read:

When the children of men descend
The oaken stairs of time,
Powers of dark will break,
The Merestone again be one.

The true ruler also shall come
To take his rightful throne;
Sore death his path shall mark,
And fire precede his reign.

Son of the High King is he called,
Ring and sorrow he bears;
But peace and joy will dawn
For the Forest he comes to free.

'I confess I do not understand more than a part of this, but it is obvious that you have come and we must start from there.'

'But are you sure it's really us who are spoken of?' Peter asked. 'Can't you have been mistaken? After all, we are only ordinary children. We've no magic powers or weapons. What can we do against this powerful witch?'

Trotter looked Peter straight in the eye. 'Elmesh does not deceive. It *is* you and inside I believe you know it is so.' He spoke with such gravity that Peter felt he could only nod in agreement. Sarah and Andrew also found their heads nodding.

'Nor will you be quite weaponless, for I have this to give you.' As he spoke, he carefully unlocked a small chest and from it drew what looked like a large powder compact covered in green tarnish. He handled the object with great reverence. 'This is Gilmere, mirror of the Merestone. It was entrusted to me by my father, Rufus the Strong. I have kept it for this day.'

He handed the object to Peter who took it gingerly.

'What do we do with it and how will it help us?' he enquired.

'If you press the clasp it will spring open and let forth its secret. But do point it away from us all and use it wisely.'

Peter held the mirror in the palm of his hand and did as he was instructed. The lid flipped open, releasing a blaze of light, the radiance of which was both terrible and wonderful. Its glare filled the room with a golden glory which made all present feel both infinitely elated and totally destroyed all at once. The sea of living light threatened to engulf them and Peter swiftly snapped the lid shut.

'Wow, that's certainly impressive. What is it?' he gasped.

Nobody rightly knows, except that it is a mirror formed by the hand of Elmesh in Elmere. That is the name we give to the enchanted glade and more particularly to the pool itself. Maybe the mirror is a shard of the Merestone or of something else. I do not know. But it has captured some of the light of the Merestone and though it has not its power it will nonetheless serve those who use it rightly in the battle against evil.'

'Why didn't Hagbane steal this too?' asked Andrew.

'Because she does not know of its existence, or at least, did not. For she has discovered many secrets from her captives since she first came. When Hagbane came she had eyes only for the jewel. Gilmere was kept hidden and, I believe, was watched over by Elmesh. My father gave it to me on his death-bed. I give it now to you to use with a true heart.'

The children gazed in awe at the innocent looking object in Peter's hand.

'Thank you for trusting us, Mr Trotter,' whispered

Sarah. 'We'll do our best to look after it and use it wisely.' She looked at her brothers, but before they could agree a blood-curdling shriek rent the air and struck a chill to the marrow of their bones. The next instant the library door crashed open and in stumbled Foxy.

'It's Hagbane!' he gasped. 'She's just down the path and she's caught Sam Squirrel. I think she's killing him! What are we going to do?'

Chapter Three

CAPTURED!

The shock of hearing such a scream and Foxy's dramatic entry left everyone stunned for a few moments. It was Peter who snapped out of it first.

'Come on, everybody,' he cried. 'Let's try and stop her.'

Before anyone could protest he was out of the door urging Foxy to show the way, rapidly followed by Aldred the stoat. Andrew and Sarah glanced at each other then ran after their brother. Trotter followed more slowly and looked extremely worried.

The three children and Foxy rushed down the forest path. The sounds of struggle grew louder and, as they rounded a bend, they came face to face with the cause of the commotion. There, standing in the middle of a small clearing, was the ugliest hag you could ever imagine. Sarah stared with horror at this vile, bent creature clothed in a long black cloak, with greasy grey hair tumbling wildly about her shoulders. Her long, distorted nose was covered in warts and her mouth twisted in a snarl of hatred. In her bony fingers she clutched a squirrel about his throat so tightly that he was rapidly choking to death. A stench of evil pervaded the air around her.

She glanced up at them with hard eyes glinting red and dropped the hapless squirrel to the ground where he lay, a limp bundle of fur, at her feet. With a snarl of rage and yet a glint of knowingness in her eyes she drew a long black wand from the folds of her cloak. There was a blinding flash and a cloud of smoke. When it cleared they found themselves paralysed. Slowly the old crone advanced and they prepared themselves as best they could for whatever awful fate she had in store for them. All except Peter, that is.

For Peter was seeing differently from the rest of the company. A strange spell had fallen upon him and before his gaze stood the most beautiful woman he had ever seen. Blonde hair cascaded over a dress of silver lace. Almond eyes and full ruby lips captured his eyes in a subtle smile. An elegant finger beckoned him, and totally entranced by her splendour, Peter walked slowly towards her.

The others gazed horrified and helpless as they saw with true eyes a hypnotized Peter walking to the horrible blackness of Hagbane. Sarah tried to cry out but found no voice to speak her warning, such was the power of the spell the witch had cast over them.

Peter, eyes fixed, reached Hagbane's side and as he did so his fingers let slip the precious mirror, Gilmere. The witch glanced down and sneered. Then, with a cackling laugh, she ground the object beneath her heel. They heard the splintering of a thousand shards of glass and poor Trotter felt his heart was breaking in pieces too.

Taking Peter's hand in her own, Hagbane led him into the depths of the Great Forest and towards her own doom-laden castle.

For what seemed like an age none of the rest could

move and then the spell began to wear off. Limbs regained their movement and tongues could again speak.

Trotter groaned. 'Oh dear, dear me. How dreadful this is! If only he had used Gilmere wisely instead of rushing out like that. And now all is lost and ruined.' He sat down on the ground, a heap of despair, his hopes as shattered as the remains of the mirror which lay at his feet.

The others stood around awkwardly and although Andrew felt Trotter was being unfair to Peter, he said nothing. At last Aldred broke the silence with a polite cough.

'Shall I round up a party to go after them, sir?'

Deep in his heart he knew this was hopeless but felt he ought to say something. Trotter shook his grey head slowly.

'No, that will not do. You will never catch her now and it would harm the boy in any case. No, let me think for a moment.'

Sarah, though she felt a worry bordering upon hysteria for her elder brother, put her arm gently around the old badger.

'Don't despair, Mr Trotter. I'm sure there's an answer. If what you say is true and Elmesh has sent us, then somehow this is all *meant*. It's got to be all right. It must be,' she said fiercely. 'We *must* get Peter back. Although goodness knows how,' she ended forlornly.

Trotter looked up into the young girl's face and smiled. He patted her hand. 'Yes, of course we must, and we will if it's at all possible. Silly me. I just felt so taken aback by the turn of events. So excited to see you and then crushed by ... by this. I'm getting old, my dear, and not used to such suddenness. You do understand, don't you?'

Sarah smiled and kissed the old badger and felt she loved him.

'Well,' he rose up as he spoke. 'I know Hagbane well enough to know that she isn't going to kill Peter, otherwise she could have done it at once. My guess is that she will use him as a hostage in some way, and that gives us a little time to plan.'

He gazed at the smashed mirror and made a decision. 'First of all, we must gather up every fragment of this, for we shall need it all tonight.'

While he performed this task, placing each piece carefully into a spotted handkerchief, the others tended to poor Sam Squirrel. Fortunately they had been in time and he was recovering from the near suffocation which he had experienced at Hagbane's hand. He gasped out that she had simply appeared from nowhere and grabbed him for no apparent reason. Aldred looked up grimly at Sarah and Andrew.

'It appears to have been a deliberate decoy to get us here. I think she knew of your coming.'

The possibility that Hagbane could read the signs too, that she could know, was more frightening than anything else. They shivered and realized that it was growing dark.

'We'd better get back to Trotter's house,' said Andrew.

They looked at the dying sun and the lengthening shadows of the gaunt trees. Then their eyes caught sight of a bright star which glittered like a globule of molten silver on the horizon and a cool hope trickled into their souls.

'El-la has risen,' whispered Trotter. 'All will be well, you'll see.'

.　　.　　*　　.　　.

High in an empty mountain pass, Oswain saw that same star and was glad. For several days he had trudged through the foothills of this mountain range until he had begun to climb a high-flung pass which he knew would bring him sight of the Great Forest. It had been then that the blizzard had struck. Visibility became almost nil as the snow beat against his face. Fierce winds seemed intent on tearing him from the path and dashing him on the rocks far below. Soon he was struggling knee deep in snow.

Almost faint with exhaustion, he had at last come through it. Now high up in the cold, clear air he saw sky again, and El-la. Beneath its light he made his crude camp, little more than a blanket and an overhanging rock. As he lay, drifting into sleep, he recalled his parting from the palace. The king and queen had not questioned his going, nor the time nor the way, for it had long been known that he should. His father had laid a firm hand on his shoulder and encouraged him to be brave. He was to send word when the task was done. His mother had gazed steadily into his eyes, her own grey eyes grave.

'Elmesh go with you, my son. Let your heart not fail, for I see not only adversaries from without but a battle that shall be within you. Yet I hope to know you shall conquer both.'

And then he had departed the security of the city with as little fuss as a man going about his daily duties.

With a yawn he settled for the night. Tomorrow he

would descend to the waste plains which preceded the Forest.

.   .   *   .   .

Mrs Trotter was one of those eminently sensible folk who turn their worry into doing the right thing at the present time as the first step to solving the thing they are worrying about. So she didn't just stand around wringing her hands. Instead, she stoked up the fire, put the kettle on and got Sarah to help her prepare something to eat. And so it was that a company who might have been pacing the room in anxiety, found themselves sitting by a cosy fire, taking their fill of tea and crumpets, and feeling greatly restored in spirits. Trotter especially was back to his old wise self.

'Before we attempt anything else,' he declared, 'we must have Gilmere repaired, for without that we are virtually weaponless.'

'But I thought it was smashed beyond all repair,' said Andrew through a mouthful of crumpet. 'How could anyone fix that mess?' He indicated the pile of twisted metal and shattered glass in Trotter's handkerchief.

'Young man,' replied Trotter, 'you will one day learn that when a work of art is broken it should be returned to its creator. He will do with it what he can. He may decide it is beyond repair and scrap it, or remake it; but that should be his decision, not yours or mine. We shall return Gilmere to Elmesh for such a ruling and I have hope that it will be repaired. And now, if you are ready, I will take you to the enchanted glade.' They nodded eagerly.

Thus the four ventured out into the night, Trotter leading the way with Aldred bringing up the rear, keeping a watchful eye open for danger. Andrew noticed that he was carrying a short sword. It was by now quite dark and Sarah and Andrew's eyes, not being as keen as the animals, were virtually useless to them so they stumbled blindly along the twisting path. Only when they came to an occasional clearing did they manage to make out the outline of dark sentinel trees.

They had no idea how long the journey was or how deep into the Forest they had gone. In fact, after some time, everything began to feel unreal. A kind of light-headedness possessed them until they thought themselves floating in a dark warm sea of nothingness. Sarah fancied she could smell exotic odours, heady scents, almost tropical in their heaviness. Surely this could not still be the petrified forest with its gloomy mosses and dormant branches. They must have floated into some other realm.

At that moment the little group broke from the undergrowth and came into the pale light of a starry night. Before them loomed great rocks outlined against the sky. The air around tingled with a feeling of life and mystery. They smelt sweet scents, carried on a warm breeze. Never had Sarah and Andrew felt so wonderfully *aware*. Trotter didn't need to tell them that they had arrived at the enchanted glade.

He led them through a narrow pass between two tall stones. Before them, under the starlit sky, stretched a lush clearing, moist and inviting. A profusion of plants were outlined in night-muted blues and greens.

'Hagbane cannot discover the whereabouts of this place however hard she tries, for, since she stole the

Merestone, a protection has fallen upon it, and though she searches for it, she does so in vain. It is the *source* you see, that is why things still grow here as in the elder days. Her magic cannot reach it. Now, come, I will take you to Elmere itself.'

Over to one side of the glade was a high, overhanging rock covered in grey-green moss. Beneath it lay a stone shelf in which was an oval pool about a metre across. As they drew near it, their feelings of awareness intensified until the very vividness of life itself threatened to overwhelm them. An intense joy filled their hearts to bursting point.

From the overhanging rock droplets of water formed themselves like pearls and fell one by one, with a bright plip into the pool below. No dewdrop glistening in the morning sun could match these droplets for silvery brilliance, for each, as it fell, caught the light of El-la and glowed as though the starlight had become encapsulated within it. Luminous shadows flickered and darted about the glade from the watery jewels. And, as each fell into the waiting pool, the observers saw that the water shone with the captured light of the ever-accumulating drops, so that it appeared to have a life of its own. The faces of the children, as they gazed in wonder, were pale and ghost-like in the light of the limpid pool. Awestruck, they said nothing.

'This is Elmere, the Star Pool, where the Merestone once lay,' whispered Trotter. 'Alas, that is no more but the pool still captures El-la's fire and it is the origin of the mirror also. We can hope that what was created here can be recreated. Pass me the pieces, Aldred, if you will.'

The stoat obliged and, with great reverence, Trotter dropped the fragments into the water. A crackling sound, like the breaking of ice, accompanied this action and blue flashes flickered in the depths of the pool.

'There, it is done. That is all we can do here for tonight. But back at home we must have a proper council of war and determine our best course.' The badger spoke with fresh resolution, his eyes sparkling behind his spectacles. The feeling was shared by each of them, and, though reluctant to leave Elmere, they were almost bouncing with hope and determination as they retraced their steps to Trotter's house. This time the children had no difficulty in seeing their way, even in the darkest depths of their meandering path.

Chapter Four

FUMBLE, MUMBLE
AND GRUMBLE

Back at the cottage they found a weasel awaiting them, who was introduced as Stiggle. He turned out to be Aldred's second-in-command and had come as soon as news of the day's events had reached him. Mrs Trotter had told him all that had happened so far.

And so the five huddled together around the fire, drinking steaming mugs of cocoa. Andrew stifled a yawn. It had been a long day but nobody was going to consider sleep just yet.

'It seems to me,' Trotter began, 'that our first object must be to rescue Peter from Hagbane's clutches. To do that we must discover his precise whereabouts in the castle dungeons, for that is where she will have taken him. Now, if you are correct, Aldred, that she somehow knew of the children's coming, you may be sure that she is formulating some evil plan, using Peter as a hostage. I do not doubt either that she will question him thoroughly about who you are. Now, Peter may be strong-willed but few can hide anything for long once they are in her grip. So our rescue attempt needs to be in earnest.'

At this point, Sarah burst into the discussion in great agitation. 'Oh, this is just too awful,' she cried.

'To think of that horrible old witch hurting Peter. Why, it's wicked! Can't we do something now? I mean, she may be questioning him and doing all sorts of terrible things. Oh, *please*, let's not just sit here talking! I want to go and get him out.'

Aldred held up a paw. 'It's not as simple as that, Sarah. For one thing, the castle is heavily guarded by Grogs and Grims, and just to charge the walls would be fatal. Most of our folk are scared even to go near the place, let alone inside. No, we must use our cunning and trust that Peter is all right, at least for the moment.'

'Okay,' said Andrew, 'I can see that, but just what are we going to do? I mean, Sarah's right in a way, it's no use just talking. I want us to do something tonight —*and* as cunningly as possible.'

'I believe there are three of the forest-folk who could discover Peter's whereabouts for us and pass the word to him not to lose hope.'

All eyes turned to Stiggle, who had sat listening thus far.

'Who are they, Stiggle?' Trotter queried.

'Why, three who are small enough to escape the guard's notice, sharp enough to find their way in and stupid enough not to be afraid. I'm thinking of Fumble, Mumble and Grumble.'

'Not those incompetent mice! You really must be joking,' exclaimed Aldred. 'Why, they can't even find their way out of their own nest without making a mess of it. Quite useless as fighting troops. Why, I remember the time when....'

'Hold on Aldred,' interrupted Trotter. 'Stiggle's idea is not so bad as it seems. Unless, of course you have a better alternative.'

Aldred thought for a moment, 'No, I don't,' he

36

admitted. 'But, let's face it, it's a bit risky, sir.'

'Risky or not, we've got to take a chance if we are to reach Peter at all. Any rescue attempt will have to be made without a hitch and that means we must know where he is and he must expect us, if we are to succeed. These three mice are our best hope as far as I can see.'

Aldred agreed reluctantly whilst Sarah and Andrew were just glad that anything was being done. So it was decided that Stiggle should fetch the three mice.

. . . * . .

During this time, life had been far from happy for Peter. The spell which Hagbane had cast over him wore off within sight of her castle and he came to himself with a start of horror as the vision of loveliness was replaced by the vile form of the witch. His arms were pinioned painfully to his sides by two evil Grogs who marched him along behind Hagbane as she strode purposefully back to her lair. Peter felt sick from the stench which arose from his captors and could not bring himself to look at their faces.

His heart sank even lower when he saw the gaunt stone fortress ahead of them. The Grogs dragged him into the gloomy portal and a massive, iron-studded oak door swung noiselessly open at Hagbane's command, though not a doorkeeper could be seen. Peter shuddered. They marched him across an open courtyard and into a large bare room where he was flung to the floor. The evil witch towered over him.

'So, what strange creature do we have here?' she grated. 'Who are you? What is your name, man-child? Answer me now, or I'll make it very uncomfortable for you.'

'Please, my name is Peter Brown,' he replied, thinking that it would be best to tell her the truth and he was an honest boy in any case. 'And I don't really know what I'm doing here, except that I came in through a hole in an oak tree.'

At this the witch's eyes gleamed. 'The old oak tree, eh? I have heard tell of this, and I do not like it. Nor do I believe you are telling me all you know. Who sent you? Why have you come to the Great Forest—into *my* domain? Eh? Answer me now!'

'Well, nobody sent us, as far as I know...' began Peter, feeling afraid, for he knew his answer would displease the witch.

'Liar!' she spat, and kicked him hard in the ribs with her pointed shoe. Peter gasped with the pain and tears came to his eyes.

'Please, it's the truth. I don't know how we got into this. All I know is what Trotter has...has told us.' His mouth dropped in dismay as he realized that he had said too much.

'So there is more? I thought so. What has that meddling old fool of a badger been up to?'

But Peter had made up his mind. He would not betray his friends. His mouth was firmly closed.

'Stubborn, eh? Well, if you want to do it the hard way, that's fine by me. I can wait. Guards, take him away! A night in the dungeons will loosen your tongue —if it doesn't, I have other ways. Think about it carefully. You will be chained up without food or water until you decide to speak.'

The Grogs dragged him down a steep flight of stone stairs into an underground dungeon. One of them lit a lantern, and then they propelled him along a fetid corridor. In the flickering light he noticed many wretched animals caged up. He was pushed into a grimy cell and his wrists tied tightly to a ring on the wall above his head so that he was stretched up on tip-toe. The door slammed shut with a dull clang of doom and Peter was left in the dark loneliness of his prison. His arms were already beginning to ache as the first wave of despair swept over him.

.   .   *   .   .

'Get out of my way, you great drip!'

The speaker was Grumble and thus he announced the arrival of the three mice in Trotter's front room. He was addressing Fumble who had just trodden on his foot and poked an elbow in his ribs in the process of getting through the door.

'Wassamarrawithyouoo, gnarrasar.' The third member of the trio was the incoherent Mumble.

'These three are aptly named,' laughed Trotter. 'And I don't think I need to tell you who is who. Fumble, Mumble and Grumble, I want you to meet Sarah and Andrew. Alas, I would have liked to be able to introduce Peter as well, but... well, more of that in a minute.'

Fumble reached out a paw to shake Sarah's hand, but somehow his arms and legs got mixed up and he finished up in a tangled heap at her feet. 'Hello,' he grinned. 'Sorry about that. It must be the uneven floor.' Sarah laughed and liked him.

'Goo evn'in nicetermetyer,' mumbled Mumble to Andrew.

'Why don't you speak up, you dimwit?' bellowed Grumble. 'Good evening, both of you. Although I don't think it is at all good at the moment. A fine to-do this is, getting me out of bed with these two idiots. It had better be something important, that's all I can say. Anyway, here we are!'

Andrew glanced at Aldred who gave him one of those 'don't-say-I-didn't-warn-you' shrugs. The children were beginning to see his point, for these really were the most unlikely spies imaginable. Even saying hello seemed to cause a minor catastrophe. Trotter, however, was quite umoved by all this.

'Now, you three mice, I have a very important and dangerous mission which I wish you to undertake for us and for which, Elmesh only knows why, you are the only ones suitable.

'Peter has been captured by Hagbane and is at present held in her castle. We want you to find your way in and to discover his whereabouts. Assuming you can do this,' (at this point Aldred gave a snort) 'I want you to pass on the message that he is to be ready for a rescue attempt. Many die for lack of hope in that accursed place, so it is extremely important that you encourage him. Is that understood?'

Mumble muttered something incomprehensible which the rest took to mean yes.

'Once you have found Peter,' Trotter continued, 'I want you to spy out the land and find the easiest way for us to get to him, if there is one, and to return to us with that information as soon as possible. We will then plan our rescue attempt.'

'Fat lot of hope I've got of even getting there with these two,' complained Grumble. 'But we'll do it for you, Trotter, if you say so. Though I don't like it one little bit,' he added.

Fumble, presumably intending to make some sort of

oration, stretched out his hand. Unfortunately, he succeeded only in knocking over a vase of dried grasses which stood on the table. Mrs Trotter shrieked as it crashed to the floor.

'My best best vase!'

Trotter groaned and Aldred lifted his paws in despair.

'Go now,' he exclaimed. 'Before you do any more damage. And good luck, because you certainly look as though you're going to need it!'

.   .   *   .   .

The three mice crouched outside the castle walls. Their approach had been unobtrusive, in spite of Fumble falling into a stream on the way and tripping over countless tree roots and Grumble's continual complaints at fate for having given him such companions. Not surprisingly, Mumble was the quietest of all.

'Now we need to find a way in,' whispered Fumble.

'Brilliant,' replied Grumble. 'Go to the top of the class!'

Mumble murmured something.

'What's that? Speak clearly for once, can't you?' yelled Grumble.

'Shush.'

They saw then that Mumble was pointing to a water waste-pipe.

'That'll do. Well done, Mumble,' said Fumble. 'Well, what are we waiting for? Come on. Shall I lead?'

'Oh no,' Grumble replied firmly. 'You'll come last. It's safer that way!'

After quite an effort they found their way out of the other end of the pipe which drained the floor of the washroom. Luckily nobody had decided to pour any water away while they were climbing up it. And so they found themselves inside the dimly-lit and evil-smelling lair of Hagbane. Very quietly (even Fumble was careful) they crept around the draughty corridors looking for any sign of Peter. For a long time their search was in vain and it was just as they were beginning to despair of ever finding him that Fumble had his lucky accident.

They were passing a floor-level window covered with an iron grating when Fumble slipped on some candle grease or tripped over a flagstone (afterwards nobody was sure which) and fell through the grating into the room below. Grumble was leading at the time and Mumble, who saw what had happened, muttered something which sounded like, 'He's filing down the widow.'

Grumble was just about to shout at Mumble when they heard Fumble call out from down below.

'I think I've found him. Down here.'

And sure enough, he was right. They had stumbled upon the basement dungeon where Peter was imprisoned. Without further delay the other two mice jumped down to join Fumble. They saw a dark figure tied to the wall.

'Psst. Are you Peter?' asked Grumble.

'Y-y-yes. W-w-who are you?' Peter answered through chattering teeth, for by now he was numb with cold.

'Never mind that for now. We're from Trotter, that's all you need to know. We've been sent to find you and to tell you that help is on its way. So don't be afraid, because you'll soon be out of here. Is there anything we can do?'

'Y-y-yes. Th-there is. C-c-can you untie my wrists or something? I don't think I can last much longer.'

The three mice scrabbled up Peter's legs and up his arms, which was an odd sensation to say the least of it, and began to gnaw at his bonds. It seemed to take ages and ages, especially as Fumble kept falling off and had to keep climbing back up again. However, at last it was done. The ropes gave and Peter collapsed onto the floor in an exhausted heap.

'Oh, thank you, thank you,' he gasped and, to his later shame, he began to cry. Actually, as it usually does, crying made him feel much better and he soon pulled himself together.

'I'm sorry about that,' he said. 'But I've made such a mess of things. Are they really going to be able to rescue me? I honestly thought I would be left here to die.'

'Yes, of course they'll get you out,' declared Grumble with somewhat more confidence than he actually felt. 'Trotter can do most things. Why, you know, he once saved my life when a Grog was chasing me and had me in a corner. So I'm sure he'll help you. We'll be back soon, so be ready.'

Mumble muttered his assent and Peter looked puzzled.

'Oh, don't worry about him,' explained Fumble. 'He never speaks clearly, but then, he never says anything very important anyway.'

Before a hurt-looking Mumble could protest, Grumble dragged them away.

'Come on, you two, we've still got to find a way for the others to get in. That drain-pipe won't do. Look after yourself, Peter. We'll return as soon as possible.'

And with that they were off, leaving Peter feeling very much better. As they left, Fumble tripped several times and brought the other two crashing down on top of him at least once. For the first time that day, Peter laughed. And then winced as pins and needles set into his hands.

Chapter Five

TO THE RESCUE!

Knowing that nothing could be done until the three mice returned, which might take some time, the company at Trotter's house decided to get some sleep. Fortunately there were plenty of spare beds as the house was often used as a place of refuge for forest-folk who were fleeing from Hagbane's troops.

Sarah snuggled down into a bed of hay and sheep's wool. She gave a deep sigh. It had been an exciting and disturbing day and also a very long one and she soon fell asleep. For a while she slept deeply, exhausted by the events of the day, but later she began to dream....

She was climbing a great tree and it seemed to go up for ever. Her legs ached as she clambered upwards into the night sky, up towards a white star which glowed in the distance. But however long she climbed it was always too far away and so she tired at last, slipped, and began to fall.

Down she tumbled until she was rolling and bouncing down a flight of dark stairs. Faces flashed before her as she fell—Trotter, Aldred, Andrew, Peter, Hagbane—each shattered into a thousand pieces before her gaze like the smashed reflection of a broken mirror. She fell into the never-ending darkness.

At last, she landed with a bump and found herself walking in the enchanted glade. The pool seemed to beckon her and she ran towards it. Deep into its waters she gazed, expecting to see her own reflection. With a shock which made her catch her breath she saw, not herself, but the face of a man staring unseeingly back at her. Before she could recover from the fright, flames consumed the whole image. And then the glade was on fire, and the Forest. Fire ran along the branches of the trees until everything was a sheet of flames. Sarah screamed and saw Sam Squirrel writhing in Hagbane's grip. Then she saw Peter's face and awoke with a start.

She lay for a while breathing rapidly in the pale light of early morning. Quietly she arose and crept from the house. The grey dawn made the Forest look even more mournful and she shivered a little in the cold. Somehow she seemed to know which way to go—a turn to the right here, left there, under this branch, across these rocks; unerringly she followed her instincts until she came to the enchanted glade.

She hesitated now, the dream still vivid in her mind. Fear and doubt possessed her and she felt no desire to gaze into Elmere. Reluctantly she approached the bowl, her heart thudding uncomfortably, and, with a supreme effort of will, she peered into the shining water and saw her own reflection. A mixture of relief mingled with disappointment flooded her being. She looked again and this time saw the mirror, Gilmere, lying perfectly whole in the bottom of the shallow pool. She reached her hand gingerly into the cold water and slowly withdrew it.

'Ah, so you have found it, have you?'

The deep voice from behind made her jump with fright, so that she almost dropped the precious mirror.

The back of her neck tingled as she slowly turned.

'Trotter!' She gasped his name with relief. 'Oh, you frightened me so! I didn't hear you coming.'

The badger smiled his apologies. 'Forgive me, my dear, but I followed you here. It is as well to be on the safe side in these days. I see that Gilmere is made well again. That is truly good news for us, for we shall need its power today, I do not doubt. Now come quickly, child, for those incredible mice should be back with news by now, if I am not very much mistaken.'

Upon their return to the house they found everybody up and about with Mrs Trotter busily supplying hot toast and marmalade to hungry mouths. And there were the three mice eagerly reporting their good news, not only that they had found Peter but had also discovered a little-used side entrance which led through a tunnel to the kitchens and dungeons. All this took some time to relate, mostly because Mumble kept adding incomprehensible bits of information through a mouthful of toast and everyone had to keep saying 'Pardon?' or 'Could you repeat that, please?' However, all were very excited and cheered by the news and by the fact that the mirror was repaired. So, as soon as breakfast was over, they prepared to commence the rescue operation.

It was agreed, after some discussion, that the mice, the children and Stiggle would make up the rescue party (no sense in having it too large) whilst Trotter and Aldred would station themselves outside the castle to deal with any pursuers once Peter was out.

Following Mumble, who by common agreement was the quietest, the party came within sight of the witch's castle. The fortress was set in a clearing but gorse bushes grew quite thickly to a distance of about ten metres from the wall on the eastern side and this provided good cover.

'Quietly now,' cautioned Stiggle. 'There are bound to be guards about.'

They crept through the undergrowth until Mumble raised a hand for them to stop.

'There's the entrance,' whispered Grumble, pointing to a round doorway which was obviously the opening to a sloping corridor. 'There are a couple of gates which we'll have to break through inside but we'll at least be under cover.'

'We shall have to take a chance and run across that open space,' said Stiggle. 'If you're ready, I'll go first.'

They all nodded and he shot out from the undergrowth, making for the doorway. But he had got no more than halfway when there was a roar and a huge and fearsome Grog stepped out from the shadow of the walls.

'Stop where you are!' he commanded, pointing his spear at Stiggle's heart. 'One move and you're dead, vermin scum.'

He advanced on the poor weasel and prodded him in the throat with the spear.

'What are you up to, you filth, and who else is with you?' he snarled.

Before Stiggle could reply, Sarah stepped boldly from the bushes, clutching Gilmere.

'Over here,' she cried.

The Grog turned swiftly to face her.

'Well now, here's a pretty catch and no mistake. Hagbane will be interested.'

He took a pace towards her and, at that moment, Sarah flipped open the mirror, pointing it towards him. Dazzling light blazed forth, triumphant and terrible. She snapped the lid shut and blinked. The Grog was nowhere to be seen.

'Oh dear. I've killed him!' cried Sarah. 'I didn't mean to.'

She felt suddenly very sick.

'No you haven't,' laughed Stiggle. 'Look, he's turned into a frog!'

And indeed, a very frightened looking frog hopped away into the bushes just as fast as his legs could carry him.

'Grogs into frogs,' Andrew chortled. 'Whatever next? That's some mirror.'

Without any further hindrance they gained the shadowy entrance to the tunnel which led into the castle. Their next obstacle was an iron gate about ten metres along the corridor. This resisted their efforts to open it in spite of there being no lock apparent.

'Here, let me have a go with that mirror,' demanded Andrew as he snatched it from Sarah's hands. 'I'll melt it down or turn it into a metal frog, perhaps. You watch!'

He opened the mirror but, although the same radiance blazed out, the door remained completely unaffected.

'Huh, that's not much good is it? Looks like it can only do one trick a day.'

It was Stiggle who spoke to Andrew. 'Young man, it's not Gilmere which is at fault, but you. Nobody shows off with Elmesh's gifts: it's not given for you to do tricks but to serve the cause of good. Now Sarah, I think you have more idea. Take the mirror, will you?'

Sarah obeyed and directed the blazing light at the gate.

Gate fast closed by Hagbane's might
Open up to Gilmere's light.

At once the door flew open and they passed through.
Andrew looked suitably shamefaced and had the grace
to say sorry to Stiggle.

'It was a bit silly of me, I suppose. I'm sorry. Seems
I've got a lot to learn from my older sister!'

Nothing more was said about the matter and they
encountered no more obstacles until they came
eventually to the outer door of the dungeons which
again gave way to Sarah's use of Gilmere. The children
stumbled forward through the vile blackness till the
mice stopped them outside Peter's cell. Peter awoke
and blinked in the mirror's sudden light.

'Andrew, Sarah. You've made it! Oh, thank goodness. And the mice. It's fantastic to see you all.'

They hugged one another thankfully.

'We're so glad to see you,' said Andrew. 'Are you all
right?'

'Yes, thanks to these mice, otherwise I'd have been
very uncomfortable by now. She tied me up to that
ring on the wall, you know.'

'The wicked old bat,' declared Sarah. 'Just wait till
we get her.'

'Well, not just yet,' said Stiggle. 'We must get out
first. Hallo, Peter, my name's Stiggle.'

Peter clasped his paw. 'It's really good to meet you,
Stiggle. Yes, you're quite right. And I don't want to
stay here a moment longer. Come on!'

'What about the other prisoners here, the forest-
folk?' asked Andrew. 'Can't we get some of them out?'

Grumble was just going to say he wondered if there
would be time when their questions were answered for

them. A key grated in the lock of the main door up the stairs.

'Quick, run for it! Run for your lives!' shouted Stiggle.

.   .   *   .   .

Hagbane had not slept that night. All through the dark hours she had paced to and fro in her den, muttering to herself, planning and plotting. This strange creature in her dungeon was a difficult problem; he was obviously from *outside*. True, she had surmised that something was up and had very cleverly caught him. But what to do now? That was the question. Should she kill him? But then he would die with his secrets. Well, she would get those out of him in the morning. Yet that still left the others. And were they all? There was more to this than met the eye. She brooded long hours over the matter.

Soon after dawn had broken, she hastened to her spell-room, an evil place filled with jars containing mysterious and obscene substances and shelves lined with books of magic. In one corner lay an object covered with a velvet cloth. Gloatingly, like a miser with his gold, she removed the covering and there lay the object of her desire, the Merestone of the Great Forest. It glowed faintly in the gloom of the den as she gazed covetously upon it.

'While this is mine I have nothing to fear,' she cackled. 'And it *is* mine, all mine. With this I shall rule for ever. No one can touch me. I shall be the greatest queen in all the universe.' Her voice rose to a screech as she stretched out her gnarled hands in a gesture of

defiance against the whole world and everybody in it.
'Mine! It's all *mine*!'

She covered the jewel, her eyes burning brightly.
With a swirl of her cloak she turned to the bookshelves,
from which she removed an old volume. Hastily
turning the pages, she came across an ancient script.

> The coming one shall come, a man set to deliver. By
> the children of men shall his path be shown. To set the
> ancient stone within its rightful sphere; to bring to life
> again the land of desolation, to....

Hagbane spat and screeched. 'I must question the
prisoner. He must know about this. I'll get it out of
him. Guards!'

A sleepy Grog came running in at her cry. He stood
shakily to attention.

'Fetch the prisoner at once,' she ordered. 'And be
quick about it or I shall turn you into a toad and boil
you alive!'

She paced restlessly up and down awaiting his
return, twisting her fingers and smacking the palm of
her hand with a clenched fist. At length the guard
returned and burst breathlessly through the door.

''E's gone, yer 'ighness. Escaped down the tunnel. I
don't know 'ow it could 'ave 'appened.'

'What!'

'I think they've only just gone, ma'am. Shall we get
after them?'

'No, fool. I shall handle this myself!'

She strode grimly from the room and began to climb
the steps which led to the top of the tower from where
she could view the surrounding forest.

The company, meanwhile, rushed from the gateway

in the wall and darted into the undergrowth. Stiggle was fastest away. The children had to go more slowly because Peter was quite weak and stiff after his ordeal. The mice stayed with them but made matters worse because Fumble succeeded in tripping them all up so that they became hopelessly entangled on the ground. And still in full view of the castle.

'You stupid twit!' exclaimed Grumble. 'I've never seen anyone...'

He was interrupted by a shrill screech from the castle. They turned to see Hagbane standing on top of the tower, her arms stretched out to the sky, holding two long wands. She looked a terrifying sight.

'Run for it,' shouted Peter. 'Never mind me.'

A chillingly cold blast hit them as they ran, numbing them to the bone. Thunder crashed and black lightning crackled from Hagbane's wand. Snow began to fall heavily, the wind blew up and moments later they were in the midst of a blizzard which blinded their eyes so that they lost all sense of direction. Soon they were struggling knee-deep through the snow and a great weariness overcame them. It became difficult to lift their leaden limbs through the biting cold.

'I don't think I can go on,' gasped Peter. 'You must keep moving. Save yourselves.'

'No, we must stick together,' Andrew cried above the howl of the wind. 'Pick up these mice, Sarah, or they'll be buried alive.'

'That's what'll happen to us all,' she groaned. 'I feel so sleepy...so sleepy...must rest....'

And with that Sarah collapsed in a heap in the driving snow. The last thing she heard was a shrill, shriek of laughter echoing across the snow from the castle tower. Then everything went black.

53

Chapter Six

THE WIZARDS' SACRIFICE

'We must get shelter,' gasped Peter as he and his brother tried to lift Sarah. 'Look, let's try to get to that tree over there.'

He indicated a spreading sycamore tree which was not so badly affected by the snow. With a supreme effort, which left them sweating in spite of the cold, they managed to drag Sarah's unconscious form to its shelter.

'Round this side, Peter. It's out of the wind and there's no snow.'

Once they were safely in the lee of the sycamore they began to feel better and Sarah stirred.

'Where am I?' she groaned. 'What's happening? Oh, my head!'

'It's all right now, Sarah. You're safe,' Peter reassured her and hugged her to himself. 'I think we've beaten that old witch's trick after all. It's certainly nice to be free again, anyway.'

Sarah smiled. Andrew jumped up and began to prance about laughing.

'Yah, silly old bat! Can't stop us. We're the great....'

At that moment everything went topsy-turvy as the ground beneath them gave way and the whole company found themselves falling in a tangle of earth, roots and bodies. Down and down they slithered until they landed in a heap at the bottom of a deep pit.

'Ooo! Ouch! Ow! What's happened?'

'Is everyone all right?'

'Is this my leg?'

'No, it's mine!'

'Oh, sorry!'

'Get your foot out of my ear.'

'I can't. I'm stuck under somebody's bottom.'

'Yeuk! I've just got a mouthful of earth.'

After much struggling and groaning, the six of them managed to disentangle themselves and take stock of their situation, which didn't seem to be too bright. They had fallen about three metres down a narrow hole and there seemed to be no way the children could climb out. Peter shook the earth off his clothes.

'Well, we're in a right fix now. It's a miracle we're all okay. We might have had all sorts of injuries. But I don't know how we're going to get out of here.' He glanced upwards.

'Do you think it's another of Hagbane's tricks?' Sarah enquired.

'Who can say?' he replied, shrugging his shoulders.

'Here, half a mo, everyone.' Andrew called excitedly. 'Look, there's a tunnel here. It got half covered in by the earth when we fell.'

They turned and saw Andrew vanish into a small hole.

'Hey, you can stand up in here,' his voice boomed. 'It must lead somewhere. Are you coming?'

'Probably back to Hagbane's castle,' moaned Grumble gloomily.

'No, it's going in the opposite direction, I'm sure,'

said Peter. 'Let's try it. It may just lead us out. We've got to do something.'

What he said made sense to the others and so, very cautiously, they began to follow Andrew along the subterranean passage. It was so dark that they had to hold on to one another and feel their way along the earth walls.

'It's a bit scary, isn't it?' Sarah whispered.

'Yes, but at least it's warm and dry.'

'And away from Hagbane.'

'We hope.'

'Oh, don't say that.'

'Sh, there's a light ahead.'

They halted, bumping into one another. Fumble got himself wrapped around Mumble's legs.

'Gerrof. Ahfortyer wera spida!'

'Quiet, you two,' ordered Peter. 'Let's go carefully now.'

The pale yellow glow was still a long way off and it took them quite a time to reach it. Everyone had lost track of how long they had been underground but their stomachs told them it was long past lunchtime when they eventually came to a left turn in the tunnel. It was from round this corner that the light came. Hearts thumping loudly, the company halted and, very cautiously, six heads peered around to see what was awaiting them.

What they saw was not very much. Just a fairly large underground chamber lit by burning torches set in brackets on the walls. The flickering light cast long shadows behind them as they emerged into the room.

'I wonder what this place is?' Peter asked.

'Well, it must belong to somebody,' answered Sarah. 'The question is, who?'

56

'Good afternoon.'

The voice was smooth and low and it made them nearly jump out of their skins. Huddling together, they turned to face its owner.

Before them stood two of the most bizarre characters any of them had ever seen. The taller one was a gaunt figure with hard features and leering mouth. He possessed a straggly black beard and moustache and was clad in a silken scarlet robe covered with a mysterious yellow design. His partner, who was very short, reminded Andrew of an egg, for he was a fat, rotund creature, totally bald, with apparently no neck. His robe of green silk was also covered in a curious pattern. He smiled a bland, oily smile and continued in his smooth low voice.

'Good afternoon. Did we startle you? I am most sorry. Welcome to our humble abode. May I ask to whom we owe the pleasure?'

For a moment, nobody spoke. It was, unfortunately, Mumble who recovered his voice first.

'Gooafnun. Weforsfolkavcomfromagbinscastwer-wiscape.'

Their hosts looked puzzled.

'Oh, shut up, cloth-head,' snapped Grumble. 'Why do you even bother? I'm sorry about that,' he addressed the strange creatures. 'What he's trying to say is that we are forest-folk and we have just escaped from Hagbane's castle. We accidentally fell into your tunnel trying to hide from a snowstorm. We're very sorry about that and don't want to inconvenience you, so, if you will kindly show us the way out, we'll be off.'

'Not so fast.' The taller one spoke for the first time. His voice grated hard and Sarah shivered slightly. 'How do we know this is true?' he continued. 'How do we know you are not friends of Hagbane come to spy on us? Who are these strange beings anyway?' He indicated the children.

Peter spoke up. 'If you please, sirs, my name is Peter and this is my brother, Andrew, and my sister, Sarah. We come from a long way away and all we really want to do is to get back to our friends. So, if you don't mind, we would be ever so grateful if you could show us the way out.'

'Quite, quite,' said the short one. He glanced at his partner. 'Only, it is a fair journey to the exit and you all look very tired and dirty. And, I should think, hungry and thirsty as well. Won't you stay and have a small meal before you go?'

The mention of food and drink made them all aware of their stomachs, especially Peter who, of course, had not eaten or drunk since they first came to Trotter's cottage.

'Well, um, yes. Yes, thank you. That really is most kind of you. Only you really will let us go soon, won't you?'

'But of course,' replied the short one smoothly. 'And now we must introduce ourselves. My name is Sorda and this is my colleague Terras. We are, um, kind of explorers into the realms of knowledge, trying to understand the secrets of the earth and heavens.'

'Oh, what we call scientists, then?' interjected Andrew.

'Scientists? Why, yes. Yes, indeed. Scientists. Now come this way, please.'

They were led through a door into another much larger underground chamber. Drawings and strange instruments littered a bench. Rolls of yellowed parchments and brown covered books lined shelves. A smell of chemicals and decay hung in the atmosphere. Almost at once Peter wished he had not accepted the invitation. It reminded him too much of Hagbane's castle.

Fumble tripped over something under the table and gasped with horror when he saw that it was a dead mouse. Lying on his back he looked up to see a whole row of mice hanging by their tails under the bench. He shivered and decided to stay well out of the way and to keep an eye on things.

'Come and sit by the fire.' Terras' invitation was more like an order and the children reluctantly obeyed.

They sat tensely before the blaze, saying nothing, until Sorda returned with a jug of steaming liquid and several metal goblets.

'Comfrey tea,' he beamed. 'Most thirst-quenching and refreshing.'

The children watched suspiciously as he filled the goblets. They waited until Terras and Sorda began to drink before savouring the brew themselves. Only Sarah just pretended to drink hers by holding it to her mouth without taking any in.

Andrew and Peter stared into the fire—and then the room began to spin. They tried to stand but found their legs could not hold them. Faster and faster the room span until they both slumped into unconsciousness.

'What have you done?' Sarah shrieked as she saw her brothers pass out. 'You've drugged them, haven't you?'

She stood angrily and faced the two wizards (for that is what they were) with her fists clenched. Grumble and Mumble dashed to her side. Slowly, eyes gleaming, their captors advanced towards them.

'Gilmere. Use Gilmere,' Grumble hissed from the side of his mouth.

'Oh! I've given it back to Peter.'

Sarah made a dash for her brother but was pounced upon by Terras who pinned her to the floor before she could make it. The two mice leapt in, followed by Sorda who grabbed them both and banged their heads together so hard that they were stunned and fell limply to the ground.

'Tie those four up,' grated Terras. 'We'll use them for experiments later. And we'll make this one the sacrifice tonight. What a stroke of luck, eh?'

Sorda gave a sinister laugh as he bound Grumble and Mumble with cord. 'Yes, this should get us nicely into Hagbane's favour and please her Grims. By the way, weren't there three mice?'

'Yes. The other one must be somewhere about. But no matter. We'll get him later. Let's deal with this one first.'

Sarah struggled and screamed as she was dragged to her feet.

'Why are you doing this?' she sobbed. 'Please let us go. We haven't done you any harm.'

Sorda smiled greasily. 'Foolish child. Did you really think we would let such an opportunity pass? We told you we experimented into all kinds of things, and here you are, creatures we have never seen before. We shall use your brothers in our studies and the mice too. But you, my dear, you are going to be offered as a sacrifice to Hagbane's Grims. That way we shall keep her happy too.'

'No, no!' She struggled in their iron grip as they dragged her up a short flight of stairs to a wooden door. Opening it, they led her outside. Before them stretched a long stone staircase, each step covered in strange symbols. Slowly the two evil wizards marched her up it. It was by then late afternoon and the sun was setting. A cold breeze blew across the darkening forest.

At length they reached a stone platform at the summit of the staircase which stretched like a grey, corrugated ribbon below them down to the yellow glare of the doorway. They lashed ropes tightly to Sarah's wrists and tied her arms above her head to two pillars on either side. Sorda drew a slender wand from the folds of his cloak and touched torches affixed to each post. Instantly, they burst into flames. The two wizards chuckled as they watched their victim writhe in the flickering light.

'Heh, heh. 'The more she struggles, the more appetising she will be!' cackled Terras.

Hearing this, Sarah ceased struggling at once. She would give no pleasure to her evil captors. And so they turned and began to descend the steps, leaving her in the gathering gloom under the flitting light of the blazing torches. She cried. She shouted. But nobody came. The door below closed with a dull thunk and, alone and helpless, she awaited her fate.

Fumble had, of course, seen all this from his hiding place under the table. And he had not been idle. His first task had been to gnaw through the cords which bound his fellow-mice, who were just coming round.

'They're going to sacrifice Sarah to the Grims,' he spoke urgently to his dazed companions. 'We've got to get Peter and Andrew awake.'

They staggered across to the collapsed forms of the boys.

'Water. Let's try water,' said Grumble.

Quickly they found a bucket and, using the goblets,

began to splash water over the lads.

'Wassamarra,' groaned Andrew. 'Ugh!'

'Wake up,' urged Fumble. 'They're going to kill Sarah.'

'What?' It was Peter who spoke. 'Kill Sarah?'

Both boys retched and were violently sick.

'Ugh! That's better. What happened? The last thing I remember was having a drink. Then everything started spinning...'

'You were drugged,' interrupted Fumble. 'Now Sarah's in great danger. We must stop those wizards.'

'Too late!'

They whirled round to see the two wizards standing at the doorway. Sorda locked the heavy door and together they strode down the staircase.

'You are too late,' continued Terras with a triumphant leer. 'She will die and so shall you.'

His callousness cleared Peter's head more effectively than the cold water.

'We'll see about that,' he cried and, leaping aside, drew Gilmere from his pocket. With a press of the clasp it sprang open and living light gushed forth like a golden spray of water. Books and parchments burst into flames under its glare. A crystal ball shattered into a thousand fragments. Apparatus melted into smouldering heaps.

'Taste Elmesh's fire!' Peter shouted.

The wizards screeched with rage but fled in fear into the tunnel as they saw the fury on Peter's face and the destruction he was wreaking.

'Now for Sarah.'

They rushed the flight of stairs and reached the locked door.

'This time I'll do it right,' muttered Peter. 'By the

light of Elmesh, let this door be broken.'

At once, to the sound of splintering wood, the oak door crumbled to firewood before the blazing light. They were outside. Ahead of them stretched the stone staircase where they could see Sarah in the torchlight. They rushed up the long flight as fast as their still-shaking legs could carry them.

'Don't worry, we're coming, Sarah,' called Andrew breathlessly.

At that very moment a shrill screech pierced the night sky. They gazed in the direction from which it had come and saw a black dot which grew rapidly in size as it plummeted towards them. Down it shot at unbelievable speed, a mighty bird with powerful wings and outstretched talons glinting in the flames from the wizards' den. Eyes glaring, it streaked towards the helpless Sarah.

Before they could react to this horror, three other cries rent the air. They turned in dismay to see other dark shapes speeding on great black wings from the direction of Hagbane's castle towards the sacrificial victim.

'Quickly, quickly!' screamed Sarah. 'Help me. Please, please help me!'

Chapter Seven

BATTLE IN THE SKY

Despair smote Peter's heart; all hope was surely gone. They were only halfway up the steep steps, lungs bursting, legs aching, and it was obviously too late. The outspread wings of the giant bird, which they now saw to be a white eagle, seemed to fill the sky above Sarah. Tears of frustration and defeat choked from him. His own sister was about to be torn to pieces! Desperately he reached into his pocket for Gilmere.

But, instead of clutching Sarah in those fearsome talons, the eagle landed beside her and tore at her bonds until she was free. Nearly faint with terror and unable to hold herself up any longer, the girl collapsed to the ground to await her fate.

Peter seized his chance and, nearly to the top of the stairs by now, flicked Gilmere open, pointing it at the bird. A blaze of light streamed forth in the gloom. The eagle seemed to grow larger and brighter in its glare. His feathers shimmered with a silvery sheen but nothing further happened. There was no burning, no destruction. The panting would-be rescuers stood amazed and beaten. And then the bird spoke. His voice was harsh and cawing and full of authority.

'I am Arca, envoy of Elmesh. I see the glory of

Gilmere is come too. It is good—but you do no good by shining it upon one who shares its nature. Close it, Peter, for you reveal too much by its light.'

A stunned Peter hesitated for a moment before obeying. All was dark again but for the flickering torches which cast eerie shadows all around them.

'Now there is little time, for the enemy has smelt blood. It is Sarah they desire, though you all must escape. I will take her to safety and deal with the foe, but you now, flee for your lives. Down the steps you will find a path to the left. It leads to the river where you will find a boat. See now, the enemy comes!'

Above them wheeled three bat-like creatures of enormous size. At an unseen signal they swooped towards the company.

'On my back, Sarah,' commanded Arca as she struggled to her feet. 'Quickly now, the rest of you. Run!'

Peter pushed the mirror into Sarah's hands. 'Here, take this and use it,' he panted. 'And look after yourself.'

She clambered onto the eagle's neck as he bent low. As soon as she was astride, the mighty wings swished the air and they were soaring aloft.

For a moment the others stood there gazing after the eagle but the sight of a Grim swooping towards them jerked each one back to reality.

'Come on, now,' yelled Peter. 'Run for it!'

Down the steps they fled, feeling a rush of cold wind as the Grim, talons bared, dived low over their heads. For once Fumble was a help for he tripped the other two mice and they tumbled together in record time to the bottom of the steps. Not that Grumble was very impressed.

'You stupid mouse,' he cried. 'Why can't you ever look where you're going?'

'Mmmggh,' agreed Mumble.

'Oh shut up!'

Before a row could develop, Peter and Andrew had pounded breathlessly down the last few steps.

'Come on, you lot, there's no time for arguing now. Look he's coming back again,' Peter called out. 'We must find that path quickly.'

Before them fire poured from the doorway of the wizards' lair and in its light they made out a dark hole through the undergrowth just to their left.

'This must be it,' cried Andrew. 'Come on.'

They scrambled in to find themselves in a low tunnel cut through dense holly bushes.

'Phew. Well, we should be safe in here,' puffed Fumble.

They looked back and could make out a monstrous bird flapping outside and screeching in fury.

'Let's not hang about,' said Peter. 'This is too close for comfort. I do hope Sarah's all right. I suppose that bird was telling the truth?'

'Nothing we can do about it now in any case,' his brother replied. 'But I think he's okay. After all, Gilmere seemed to make him glow. I think he must be on our side.'

Peter nodded. 'Well, come on then. Let's find that boat. I wonder how far away it is?'

.   .   *   .   .

Sarah had never experienced anything like it in all her life—the feeling of immense power as Arca's tremendous wing-thrusts lifted them ever upwards; the rushing sound of the wind past her ears, tearing at her clothes; the dizzy view of the Forest below her as they whirled into the twilight sky. It was breathtaking and scary too. She clutched tightly at the eagle's neck.

Suddenly, Arca let out a wild screech of primeval fierceness. The three Grims had joined battle with them and now circled menacingly, shadowy vultures of death outlined against the pale afterglow of early evening. One swooped in close, fangs snapping and talons outstretched, seeking to tear Sarah from her feathery perch. But Arca was quick and strong and easily outmanoeuvred his enemy. The other Grims tried the same attack with equal lack of success.

As Arca continued to lead the Grims a merry dance, Sarah's confidence grew. The eagle's back was warm and secure and the thrill of battle began to stir in her. She remembered then that Peter had given her Gilmere and, gripping tightly with her knees, took it in her hands.

'Enough of this,' cawed Arca and whirled upwards in a steep climb. He turned in mid-flight and plummeted like a stone towards his enemy below. Sarah clung to his neck and flipped open the lid of Gilmere. Light streamed forth and before Arca's claws could strike, the Grim beneath them shrivelled to a cinder and was no more. Arca blinked.

'You deny me my prey, Sarah, but I do not begrudge it you, for they are merciless creatures.'

The two remaining Grims closed in fast, one from above and one from below. Arca streaked across the sky as they homed in on their target. Sarah gritted her teeth as the moment of impact rushed towards them. Then, with astonishing skill and enormous strength,

Arca threw open his wings and stopped in mid-flight. The move was too much for the Grims and they hurtled headlong into one another, colliding with a mighty crash of skin and bone. One dropped like a stone into the trees far below, mortally wounded. The other, sensing defeat, quickly recovered, turned, and flew hard and low back towards the sanctuary of Hagbane's castle.

'We shall not let this one escape,' cried Arca as he set off in rapid pursuit. 'Death to the enemies of Elmesh!'

Although fear propelled the Grim at great speed, the eagle was faster and the gap closed rapidly. Sarah opened the mirror and tried to focus the beam on the foe but could not do so. It looked as if he would gain the castle. Indeed, they were right over the ramparts when Arca struck. His talons sank into the Grim's neck. With a horrifying screech the creature writhed and fought to shake off its pursuer. Sarah clung on desperately as the giants fought. At length Arca executed a death-blow and the Grim fell mangled to the courtyard beneath.

Arca began to climb at once but hardly a moment too soon for a crackle of fire leapt forth from the wand of a furious Hagbane who had watched all from her castle ramparts. She screamed with rage as the fiery bolt merely singed the tail feathers of the victor. Sarah saw her white face contorted in hatred, her clenched fists shaking angrily as they made their escape.

'Phew, that was close,' she gasped.

'Yes, but we are safe now,' the eagle replied as he climbed away into the night. 'Now I must take you to a place of rest and refreshment, that you may renew your strength.'

The excitement over, Sarah suddenly felt very weak and sick. She closed her eyes and, nestling against the eagle's back, sank into oblivion.

.   .   *   .   .

While all this had been taking place, Peter and Andrew and the three mice had been struggling in pitch darkness along the secret path. It turned out to be an extremely muddy and tortuous route through a tangle of holly, hawthorn and gorse bushes, and the two boys had to be bent double most of the time. As the path plunged downhill, the muddiness increased, until they were slithering rapidly along through the clawing prickles. Consequently, when they eventually emerged by the riverside, they were thoroughly exhausted and miserable.

'Gosh, I thought that would never end!' exclaimed Andrew. 'I wonder where we are now.'

'Anywhere's better than back there,' Peter replied. 'I hope Sarah's all right, that's all. I wonder when we'll see her again, and Arca, too, for that matter.'

'It's a good job he came when he did. I wouldn't have fancied our chances against those black beasts. I'm sure Arca has saved Sarah. He didn't look as though he needed anyone to look after him.'

'Hm, I wonder where those two evil wizards have gone as well.'

'Well, not back to their lair, that's for sure. You certainly put an end to that,' laughed Andrew.

'What fools we were to be taken in by them. Just think what might have happened to us all!' Peter shivered at the thought.

Their conversation was interrupted by a call from Grumble.

'Hey, we think we've found the boat. Over here.'

They followed the direction of his voice until Andrew tripped over Fumble and fell with a loud *splat* on to the muddy ground.

'Ouch, who was that? As if I couldn't guess. Where are you?'

'Over here.'

In the darkness they could just make out the shape of a small rowing boat and hear the sound of running water. They crowded round it.

'Do you know where we are?' Peter queried.

'We know this river. It's the Wendle,' answered Fumble. 'It should be possible to get back to Trotter but at night time everything looks so different. I'm not sure I'll recognize when to stop.'

'And we can't afford to make a mistake because it goes fairly close to Hagbane's castle,' added Grumble. 'And I for one don't want to go back there.'

'Nor me,' said Peter with feeling. 'That settles it then, wizards or no wizards, Grims or no Grims, we're staying here tonight. I'm too tired to go on, anyway. Does anyone think differently?'

Nobody did and so the five of them clambered into the boat, which fortunately was dry, and snuggled up together for warmth as best they could. Before long, the drama and exhaustion of the day overtook them and they fell fast asleep. Nothing stirred as they slept beside the dark-flowing river beneath the severe gaze of the moon and stars.

Chapter Eight

THE FAIRY QUEEN

Before him stretched bleak moorland, behind, the
inhospitable mountains. Somewhere, as yet out of
sight, lay the Great Forest and his strange destiny.
And so Oswain tramped all day across the scrubby
grass and pitiful heather which made up the waste
plains west of the Forest. The keen wind and dull sky
had matched his mood. For, even if victory is assured,
the anticipation of fierce battle does not make a man
jubilant so much as give him a certain grimness of
outlook. And this the more so for Oswain, for he knew
only a part of what lay before him.

In such a frame of mind he marched the day through
until, at length, he came within sight of the Great
Forest, a dark swarth of wintery trees stretching across
the horizon, and before it the serpentine silver thread
of the River Wendle.

'Tomorrow, I shall enter and see what shall befall
me,' he breathed.

. . * . .

A cold, pale dawn awoke the company in the boat; the
cheerless trees stood stark in the new day's light.

'Brr, it's cold,' shivered Andrew, his teeth chattering as he arose.

'Oof! Ouch! Oh, my leg, it's stuck,' Peter grunted. 'Gosh, I do feel stiff. Ouch!'

Slowly and lazily the three mice uncurled themselves.

'Reckon they slept better than us,' Andrew laughed ruefully. 'Ow, my neck doesn't half hurt. I wonder what time it is?'

'No idea, but we must get back to Trotter as soon as possible. They'll be worried sick about us. Come on, you mice, wakey wakey!'

'Go away,' groaned Grumble. 'Give us some peace and quiet.'

'Grummffn,' added Mumble.

'Breakfast-time,' Andrew called—and in an instant all three were awake. 'Egg, chips, baked beans and bacon.'

'Oh, shut up, you're only making me feel even hungrier,' complained Peter. 'Come on, everyone. There's no breakfast until we get back to Mrs Trotter's. Plenty of water, though!'

'I wonder what sort of night Sarah had. Probably she's tucking into eggs and bacon at the Trotters' right now. Lucky thing!'

'Well, we'll soon be there too, I hope,' Peter replied. 'By the way, keep an eye open for those two wizards. I somehow don't think we've seen the last of those nasties. I still can't get over how we were so taken in by them. I felt something was wrong the moment we met them, you know, but I ignored the feeling.'

'It never does to do that,' said his brother. 'Anyway, the quicker we get moving, the further away we'll be from them. Come on, everyone, let's get this boat into the water.'

'Wait for us, we're ready,' grumbled Grumble who felt cheated out of his breakfast.

And so together they heaved and shoved until the boat slid with a slight splash into the water.

'Say, hold on to her or she'll float away,' cried Andrew. 'Grab that rope, quick!'

He pointed to a rope trailing from the prow. Fumble, who was nearest, leapt for it and caught the end. Unfortunately, he caught his feet too and found himself being dragged along the bank in a complete tangle as the boat drifted downstream.

'Ow! Help! Ouch!' he cried.

The others chased after him and just managed to prevent him being dragged into the water.

'Stupid clot!' exclaimed Grumble. 'That nearly cost us the boat. Then where would we have been?'

'Walking, I suppose,' retorted Fumble. 'Oh, my head hurts!'

'Don't you....'

'Hey,' laughed Peter. 'Come on, you two. We've got the boat, so all's well. Hop in now.'

Soon they were drifting pleasantly with the current. The sun had risen and the air felt surprisingly warm, almost spring-like. For a little while they were able to forget their worries and cares and bask in the sunshine as the water lapped and gurgled merrily around the boat and the banks slid by.

For a good deal of their journey the trees came right down to the water's edge but every so often a small grassy clearing broke the monotony. One of these had a land-mark indicating the path to Trotter's house. So they took it in turn to watch out for it.

'Loo prittyflors.'

Mumble tugged at Peter's sleeve. He was pointing at a clearing ahead of them on the left bank. Peter heaved himself up from the bottom of the boat where he had been lying and everyone crowded to see what Mumble was pointing at. Nobody, of course, had understood what he had said.

'Now, look,' cried Peter. 'Those are flowers, I'm sure.'

'We've not had flowers in the Forest for many years,' said Fumble. 'This is most unusual. We must stop and look. I wonder what it means?'

The object of their gaze was a patch of bright yellow which glowed like a jewel in the morning sun, contrasting sharply with the drabness around. But as they drew closer it became apparent that the flowers were not flowers at all but something even more amazing.

'Why, they're alive,' exclaimed Peter. 'They, they're moving. I think they're fairies!'

And, sure enough, there were dozens of little yellow figures prancing about on the grass in the sunshine. The light glistened off their gossamer wings and happy laughter accompanied their dancing. A sweet, heady scent wafted over the entranced onlookers and they perceived that it came from giant yellow puff-balls which the fairies were tossing to one another. Every so often one would burst in a shower of scented yellow dust which the breeze carried towards them.

Peter pushed the tiller over until the boat ran lightly aground on the bankside. As soon as they came to rest, a fairy, who was taller and of greater splendour than the rest, emerged from the midst of the dance. She wore a magnificent daffodil-yellow robe edged with gold and a golden crown was set upon her blonde hair.

She walked with grace and poise towards them.

'It must be the queen of the fairies,' whispered Andrew.

'Hail, travellers,' she cried in a sweet, musical voice. 'Welcome to you on this fine morning for dancing!'

'Er, um, hello,' stammered Peter, unsure of how you addressed a fairy queen. 'Er, excuse me, but you . . . you are fairies, aren't you?'

The queen replied with a tinkling laugh. 'Why, yes, indeed we are. And I am their queen. And you? Pray tell me who you are?'

'Well, we're travellers, actually, though we're not going too far. We're looking for the path which will lead us to Trotter the badger. Do you know where it is?'

'Why, yes, of course. It's around the next two bends in the river. But what brings you this way in the first place, pray?'

Andrew spoke. 'If you please, ma'am, we've just escaped from two wizards and a great eagle rescued our sister. That was last night. So we're trying to meet up together.'

'Then have you not eaten?' the queen queried.

'No, not a thing, your highness,' replied Grumble.

The queen clapped her hands. At once, two fairies came forward bearing a golden goblet filled with a clear liquid.

'Drink this,' she invited. 'It is a magic nectar which will refresh you and give you strength for the rest of your journey.'

Peter remembered his mistake of the night before and hesitated. Seeing this, the queen laughed gaily.

'Ah, you think it may be poisoned, do you? I assure you, by Elmesh himself, it is not. See for yourself.'

So saying she took a deep draught. Grumble agreed to have a sip and, on so doing, pronounced it very good. So they all drank of the liquid which turned out to be intoxicatingly delicious. At once, as the fairy queen had promised, they felt better. The events of the day before and the uncomfortable night in the boat, all began to fade like a nasty dream. Peter pushed the boat back in the water and, waving cheerfully to the fairies, he jumped in as it began to drift on its journey once more.

'Farewell, brave travellers,' called the queen after them as she waved goodbye.

'Bye, bye, dear fairies, thank you,' sighed Peter, who now felt warm and relaxed. He flopped down in the boat and closed his eyes. 'Keep an eye open for the second bend, won't you?'

Fumble had never felt so confident before; he walked all the way around the rim of the boat without falling once and finished up balancing on the prow on one paw.

Mumble addressed the crew with perfect diction: 'My dear fellow-mice, yeomen amongst the forest-folk, and Peter, and Andrew, children of men and fair visitors to our realm. What a grand company we are! The wizards are defeated, the Grims too and so shall the wicked Hagbane be also. Nothing shall stop us, gentlemen.'

He sat down to applause from them all, especially Grumble who clapped and cheered and finally burst out laughing! The effect was contagious and soon all five were doubled up in the bottom of the boat, hooting with laughter until their sides ached. Which is why none of them looked back.

For if they had, the sight would have sobered them

up instantly. Where the bright fairies had danced there remained nothing but a black, stinking patch of rotting weeds and the fairy queen was no more than a bent slimy stalk.

The whole thing had been a delusion created by Hagbane herself. Back in her castle she gloated over her crystal ball in which she had seen everything.

'Heh, heh,' she cackled. 'Fools! Meddling brats! It worked even better than I expected. I shall destroy them now, once and for all. Heh, heh, heh!'

Her laughter continued and the sun passed behind the clouds. Still quite intoxicated by the magic nectar, the company in the boat failed to notice that the river was beginning to flow faster and more turbulently. They also missed the land mark which indicated the path back to Trotter's house. The little boat began to bob and buck in the swirling foam and was soon racing along while the crew, who were now resting from their hilarity, were quite oblivious to the fact that matters were fast getting out of control.

The reason for this change of speed was soon revealed for, having rounded the two bends, the boat began to career along a straight stretch of river which led directly to a rocky waterfall. Faster and faster it bobbed, like a cork, caught helplessly in the surging current. Jagged rocks and boulders jutted from the river bed and soon there was a sickening crunch as the boat crashed into one of the rocks. Water poured over the bows, dowsing the merry crew in the bottom, as the current hurled the boat forward again.

The effect of this sudden cold soaking was to bring them instantly to their senses. Peter scrambled up and peered over the edge. He gasped with fright as he saw the menacing rapids through which they were rushing and the apparent end of the river right ahead of them.

'Quick, everyone,' he yelled. 'We're heading straight for a waterfall!'

The boat crashed and ricocheted off the rocks and shot towards the brink. The crew covered their faces, expecting the worst, when there was another crash and their craft jammed fast between two boulders right on the edge of the falls. It hit the rocks so fast that Fumble was thrown overboard and would have been swept to his doom if his leg had not caught once more in the rope. He gurgled and spluttered, choking in the foam and spray. Quickly, the others grabbed the rope and hauled him back on board, a dripping, sorry sight.

The boat creaked and groaned beneath them and was rapidly filling with water. It was quite obvious that it would soon break up and that, unless help came, they were lost. The hissing roar of the waterfall drowned out all possibility of conversation so Peter indicated that they could do nothing except shout together for aid.

'Help! Help!' they cried. 'Somebody please help us!'

Chapter Nine

SAFE AND SOUND

The warmth of the morning sun woke Sarah from an untroubled sleep. Lazily, she opened her eyes, squinting against the sun's glare. She smiled dreamily and her hand felt the softness of the sheepskin rug on which she lay. For a long moment she imagined she was in her own bedroom back home.

Then it all began to come back to her—the flight from Hagbane's castle, the awful wizards, how she had felt when Arca descended upon her, that tremendous battle against the Grims—and then, her mind was a blank. She didn't know what had taken place after that. Where was she? She sat up with a jolt and gazed around her. To her astonishment she was lying near the entrance of a small, sunlit cave high up on a rocky precipice. Before her stretched a breathtaking view of the Great Forest, of silvery rivers and of purple mountains in the hazy distance. The air smelt fresh and invigorating and she breathed deeply. 'Arca must have brought me here,' she thought to herself. 'I wonder where he's got to?'

Gingerly, she arose and made her way to the cave entrance. The sight made her gasp, for below her the rock fell sheer away to a dizzy depth beyond her imaginings. She hastily retreated, realizing that she was very high up a mountain and only Arca could remove her. As she retraced her steps, she noticed for the first time a bowl of clear liquid and a lump of bread. It reminded her that she had not eaten or drunk for a long time so she quickly tucked in, thankful to Arca for his thoughtfulness. The liquid tasted sweet and tangy and, whatever it was, it had an invigorating effect on her, so much so that she began to sing for joy. She flopped back upon her sunlit bed to await Arca's return. Such was the sense of pure goodness which pervaded her that she felt not a care in the world. She decided to call the drink 'Arca-ade'.

.　　.　　*　　.　　.

Far, far below and on the opposite side of the Great Forest, Oswain came to the banks of the River Wendle. There he found the ford and crossed from the barren waste plains into the shadows of the tall trees, his arrival unnoticed by any except those trees, some of which seemed to tremble at his coming.

'My journey is almost ended and my destiny about to begin,' he announced to the silent woods. And so saying, he plunged into the depths of the Forest.

.　　.　　*　　.　　.

'Help, somebody rescue us,' cried Peter. 'Help!'

The water continued to crash and roar about them and another piece of the boat snapped off with a splintering sound to be carried over the falls to the rocks below. By now they were all soaked to the skin, what with the spray and the water which more than half-filled their disintegrating boat. Andrew wondered how long they could last out for already he was growing numb with cold and his teeth were chattering. Peter reckoned the boat had only minutes to survive before the crashing water smashed it to matchwood. He called out even more earnestly.

Then, just as they were beginning to feel all hope gone, a voice called from the bank.

'Hold on. We'll soon have you out of there. Don't worry. Just hold on.'

'It's Trotter!' Andrew shouted. 'Hurray! And look, there are lots of other animals with him.'

They followed his gaze to see a large contingent of the forest-folk waving to them from the riverside. They waved back excitedly.

'But how are they going to rescue us?' bellowed Peter above the roar of the falls.

'I don't know, but Trotter seems pretty confident he can do it,' his brother replied. 'Look, he's arranging something or other.'

The next moment they saw a fluttering of black wings and, to their surprise, several blackbirds began to fly across the intervening water. And dangling from their claws was a length of rope.

Peter laughed. 'Fantastic! Look at that. It's a life-line.'

The rescue was a marvellous piece of teamwork. The blackbirds dropped their line into the eager hands of the boat crew and Trotter called out instructions from the bank. The mice might have been hauled across together but nobody wanted to risk being with Fumble in case he messed it up and Grumble refused to go with Mumble in case they didn't understand one another properly! So, the crowd on the bank heaved away at the rope and dragged the mice across individually. As each landed in a soggy heap of fur he was surrounded by well-wishers, while the blackbirds flew off with the rope for the next one.

'Our turn now,' Peter shouted. 'You go next, Andrew. No, don't argue; we haven't much time before this thing breaks up. Go on!'

After a moment's hesitation, Andrew plunged into the icy current, the chill fairly taking his breath away. For one awful moment it looked as if the forest-folk would not be strong enough to pull him out and he would be swept over the top. Their determination, however, was such that, after a lot of heaving and blowing, he reached the shore safely.

'Get the rope to Peter. Quick!' he gasped.

They were only just in time, for, with a final sickening crunch, the boat broke into pieces and disappeared over the falls. Peter clutched desperately at the rock and managed to grab hold of the rope. His journey through the raging torrent was easier than Andrew's because Andrew was able to pull as well. And so they all reached dry land in safety, and joined their friends.

'Thank you, thank you, Trotter,' Peter panted. 'And everyone. Thank you so much. You turned up just in time.'

'But how did you know?' Andrew asked. 'Did you hear us calling?'

'All in good time,' replied Trotter. 'The first thing to do is to get you home and dry with something to eat. You have done very well, all of you. I feel extremely proud of you. Now, let us hasten back. No more questions until we've had some of Mrs T.'s cooking, eh, Andrew?'

So it was that three-quarters of an hour later they were gathered around a blazing fire in Trotter's home, drinking tea following a splendid meal. The boys and the mice were feeling much better and had nearly dried out after their ordeal.

'Now then, Trotter, please tell us what has been happening and how you found us,' requested Peter.

'Very well,' replied the old badger. 'Aldred and I waited for a long time after you had entered the castle but nothing happened. We began to fear the worst and think you had fallen into a trap when we saw Hagbane in her tower magicking up that snowstorm. We knew then that you must have been successful and so tried to find you, but the storm was so bad that we could not. We searched for hours until it was quite dark but even our best trackers could find no trace of you, what with the snow.'

'That's because we were underground by then,' interrupted Andrew and proceeded to tell them of Terras and Sorda and their escape.

'Ah, that's how it happened, is it? No wonder we couldn't find you.'

'Did you know of those wizards?' asked Peter.

'Rumours had reached us of some mischief afoot.' It was Aldred who spoke. 'Forest-folk have been disappearing without trace and those Grims have been seen flying at dusk, but we had not realized the connection until now. It's utterly awful.'

'I agree,' added Stiggle. 'If I ever get my hands on those two....'

'Well, to continue,' Trotter interrupted. 'We kept searching, hoping to find a clue and then the great eagle, Arca, came. He told us what had happened and advised us to get some rest. He returned this morning to help us in the search. The eye of one such as Arca misses little and he directed us to the waterfall. He had seen your plight.'

'I still don't quite understand what really happened on the river,' said Andrew. 'All I know is, we met some fairies and the next thing I remember is the waterfall.'

'That is not too difficult to explain,' Trotter answered. 'You were the victims of one of Hagbane's tricks. There are no fairies in the Forest but she created a delusion which fooled you all and took away your control of the boat. As far as she is concerned it was a good way to destroy you.'

'And she very nearly did,' said Peter glumly. 'What a fool I was to be taken in twice.'

'You weren't the only one,' his brother consoled him. 'We were all fooled this time. Just thank goodness for Arca's help.'

'Evil has often copied good, young man,' said Trotter seriously. 'Do not trust to appearances or words, especially smooth and flattering words. Remember too, Peter, that a thing of great evil can also be a thing of beauty; nor are ugly things necessarily bad. You must learn to see the inner-ness of things and especially of people, if you would be wise.'

Aldred continued. 'Arca is a good example of this. He frightens me, to tell you the truth, and he's a strange creature, living in a high and lonely world, where he holds his own counsels. But he's altogether good and he is a messenger of Elmesh. He'll return to us soon—and with Sarah. Oh, she's all right, you know. Perfectly safe with Arca, she is, even if he does scare me.'

Peter and Andrew were delighted to know that their

sister was safe and were thrilled to have a report of the aerial battle against the Grims and the part she had played in it. They almost wished they had stayed behind to watch—until they remembered the Grim which had so nearly struck them.

As they all relaxed and talked, the mice became drowsy in front of the fire and fell fast asleep, curled up on top of one another.

'They were marvellous,' laughed Peter, looking at them. 'You were right, Stiggle, they were the ideal choice.'

Stiggle smiled towards Aldred, who grudgingly agreed. Trotter suddenly became serious.

'Listen,' he said. 'All this worries me. I do not pretend to know all that Elmesh is doing, and, doubtless, he has good reason for sending you children here, but it is also obvious to me that, even with Gilmere, you are no match for Hagbane.'

'I agree,' said Peter. 'I feel completely out of my depth in all this. Sorry about the pun, Andrew! But it's true, and what with Terras and Sorda to deal with as well, I don't know quite what we're to do. It's clear that they're all prepared to kill us.'

'We do have Arca on our side,' his brother reminded him.

'He is quite a fighter,' said Aldred. 'But I doubt if even he could beat Hagbane single-handed. Trouble is, so many of our best fighters are locked up in her castle. If only we could rescue them.'

'I know,' said Peter. 'I saw some of them. They looked pretty well beyond hope. I'm only sorry that we couldn't rescue any. We must find a way to get them out.'

'We need help,' Trotter declared. 'I don't know

where it is to come from, but I shall enquire of Elmesh tonight. I cannot risk you children's lives again. Things are too unevenly matched at present and until matters change I think we must simply lie low and keep out of harm's way as best we can. Though, goodness knows, she will be out hunting us soon enough.'

They sat glumly together, brooding over the problem. Nobody really knew what to say and the longer they sat the more oppressive the enemy seemed. A black cloud of despair settled over their souls.

All of a sudden there were noises outside: a heavy footstep, a cracking twig. They jumped as the sounds broke their silence. Slowly, the door swung open with a light creak of the hinges. A long black shadow fell across the floor. Stunned, Mrs Trotter screamed and dropped her teacup.

Chapter Ten

OSWAIN TAKES CHARGE

Fear and dismay paralysed them as they stared at the long shadow which darkened the threshold. Surely Hagbane had come in person to wreak her vengeance. Slowly, they lifted their eyes as the shadow moved.

But it was no evil-looking Hagbane who entered the room a moment later. Instead, they found themselves confronted by a tall stranger dressed in a hooded, green travelling cloak. For a moment, they hesitated and then Aldred whipped out his sword. If this was not Hagbane, presumably he was one of her allies.

'Show yourself,' growled the stoat, 'before I run you through.'

The stranger laughed and threw back his cowl. Before them stood a man of handsome features, stern yet kindly, mature and yet alert with the fire of youth.

'There will be no need for that, Aldred.' His voice was rich and deep. 'Allow me to introduce myself. I am Oswain, the Son of the High King of the West.'

He smiled and bowed slightly. There was an authority in his manner, and a fearlessness, which made Aldred lower his sword. The stranger looked about him.

'Ah, you must be Peter and you, Andrew. Yes, and

you are Trotter, noble lore-master of the forest-folk, if I am not mistaken. To you, I offer my apologies for having entered your house unannounced, but I felt such discretion was wise.'

He turned to Mrs Trotter. 'And my special apologies to you, dear lady of the house, for causing you such fright. Please forgive me.'

'Well, I'm sure I do, sir,' replied a flustered Mrs Trotter.

'That's fine and well,' Aldred spoke again. 'But isn't it time you explained yourself a bit more? Like, for instance, who sent you? Who's side you are on? Why you're here? And how come you know so much about us?'

The tall stranger smiled. 'Of course. You are quite right and I will do so, but first, may I put you all at ease by saying that I have come to the Great Forest at the bidding of Elmesh himself.'

'If that is so, you are truly welcome,' said Trotter. 'But you will understand our caution when I tell you that our enemy is a skilled mistress of deception and we have had much sore experience of that in recent times. To say you are from Elmesh is a strong statement, my friend. What proof do you bring?'

'I give you first my oath that it is so and I do so by the fire of the Merestone and by the light of El-la. But, more tangibly, I reveal this to you.'

He removed his glove and showed them a ring upon the second finger of his right hand. The ring was large and of intricately fashioned gold, but what caught their attention was the jewel set within it. For this was no ordinary diamond or emerald; this did not catch light and reflect it. It contained its own light which smouldered at the mention of the Merestone. Trotter inspected it closely, gazing in awe and wonder.

'Yes, you surmise correctly,' said the stranger, without waiting for Trotter to speak. 'It is of the same kind as the Merestone, for it is a piece of that jewel itself.'

'Sit down, please,' whispered the old badger. 'I need no further proof. For one who has gazed upon the Merestone, it is enough. It is enough.'

Once they were all seated Oswain began to answer their questions.

'Long years ago I was given this ring by my mother. She would not say how she came by it but I remember feeling that it had cost her much suffering to obtain it. Never has it been removed from my hand and nor could it be now, as you can see. Yet it is to be removed for it is spoken that this jewel shall again be reunited with the Merestone, the manner of which I do not yet know.'

'The prophecy,' interrupted Peter looking eagerly at Trotter. 'The one you showed us.'

'Yes,' Trotter nodded. 'It is so. Then you, Oswain, are the promised ruler, the coming one who shall set the Great Forest free. And I was not mistaken concerning the signs, nor with regard to the children. Elmesh be praised! Sire, I am your servant and at your command.'

He bowed low before Oswain and the others followed suit.

'I'll put the kettle on,' said Mrs Trotter. 'It's not every day we have royalty in our home.'

Oswain smiled at her. 'If you but knew it, Mrs Trotter, you are of royal blood yourselves for true nobility is not by birth but is of the very soul of the true-hearted.'

Mrs Trotter suddenly felt embarrassed and hurried out to make the tea.

'Are you aware, sir, of the whereabouts of the Merestone at this time and of the dreadful plight which is ours?' asked Stiggle.

'I know of that and my destiny involves the recovery of the stone and the destruction of the forces of darkness which oppress you. I fear it shall be a hard battle but it will be won. Do not doubt that.'

'Did Elmesh tell you all our names too?' queried Andrew.

'No. There is a very simple answer to that question. I have spoken with Arca already. He has told me much.'

'Arca! Of course. And Sarah. Is Sarah all right?'

'She is very well, as you will see for yourselves quite soon. We have already met briefly. So come now, let us meet properly.'

So saying, he led the company outside and, gazing up into the sky, uttered a long shrill whistle. For a moment nothing happened and then they spied a black dot high among the clouds. It grew rapidly as Arca plummeted to the earth. Great wings outspread, he landed a few feet away from them. And there was Sarah clutching his neck.

'Sarah!'

'Oh, Peter, Andrew, thank goodness you're safe! Oh, I'm so glad to see you again!'

She slipped from Arca's back and threw her arms around her brothers. For a while they had no words to express their feelings but after that there was no stopping them.

'I've been to the most marvellous place, a cave in the mountains. The view was fantastic.'

'What's it like riding on Arca's back?'

'Did you really kill a Grim yourself?'

'Isn't Oswain smashing? We met him earlier this afternoon. What do you think he's going to do?'

At that moment Mrs Trotter came to the door with a tray of steaming mugs.

'What a to-do,' she exclaimed. 'I come into the front room and you've all gone. And there I am standing here with all these cups of tea to drink. Sarah! You're back, my dear. Here serve these somebody while I give her a kiss.'

Peter went over to Arca.

'I want to say thank you for saving Sarah's life and, well, all of us really. You've been absolutely marvellous.'

'Elmesh has sent me to play my part in the destruction of evil. He has sent you too. It was right that we met. I was glad to be in time,' croaked the eagle in reply.

'Yes, well, thank you anyway,' Peter replied, a bit nonplussed.

'You must not mind Arca's ways,' said Oswain. 'He is one who inhabits harsh and lonely places. He does not feel as we do, except to do the will of Elmesh. That is his joy. Now I must speak with him for a little while, for one such as he will not enter the confines of a house and we have to make plans tonight. So please excuse us for a while.'

.   .   *   .   .

The rest of that afternoon was spent in earnest conclave as the group discussed how they might defeat Hagbane.

A new determination and confidence filled their hearts now that Oswain was amongst them. No one now questioned his right to leadership in the campaign, and he largely directed their discussions.

'We need to be wise,' he said. 'For it would be no victory if Hagbane escaped with the Merestone. We must recapture that at all costs.'

This rather put paid to Andrew's suggestion that they should simply blow her up in her castle, assuming that they possessed explosives—which they didn't! Something more subtle was needed.

Aldred spoke up. 'It seems to me that we must rescue the prisoners before we do anything else. Some of my finest troops are in her dungeons and she will certainly kill them if she once suspects an attack. In fact, I should think they're at great risk even now after recent events.'

'Yes, and she can always blackmail us while she has them. Their lives for her terms,' added Stiggle.

'I agree,' answered Oswain. 'That must be our first priority. Now we need to find a way of drawing her and the guards away from the castle. We must find her weak spot.'

'Oh, that's easy enough,' said Trotter. 'She is vain. The most self-conceited creature you could ever imagine.'

'She might be vulnerable to a bit of flattery then. Hmmm.'

'In that case, I think I have a plan.' It was Stiggle who spoke. Carefully, he explained to them his ideas.

'It might work. It might just work!' cried Oswain jubilantly.

.   .   *   .   .

That night saw much unaccustomed activity on the part of the forest-folk. Animals scurried hither and thither in the darkness and there was much whispering of instructions and passing on of progress reports. It was not until that cold dark hour before the dawn that most fell tired but satisfied into their beds. Indeed, if it had not been for sheer exhaustion many would have stayed awake with excitement. However, they needed their rest in order to be completely alert for the events to come.

.　　.　　*　　.　　.

Stage two of Stiggle's plan began quite early that morning when Fumble, Mumble and Grumble, who had been excused the night work (to the relief of many!), set off once more in the direction of Hagbane's castle. Only this time they made no attempt to conceal their coming.

'Ouch, that hurt my toe,' groaned Fumble as he picked himself up after tripping on a tree root.

'Huh, if you carry on at this rate we'll never even reach there,' Grumble complained. 'Not that that would be a bad thing, if you ask me. Why does it always have to be us who get landed with the dangerous jobs, that's what I want to know? I mean, just as likely she'll kill us on the spot after the trouble we've caused her.'

'Ohstopmoanin.'

'What's that you say, Mumble? Eh? Speak up then.' Grumble was feeling very moody indeed.

'Leave him alone,' said Fumble. 'I'm sure it'll be all right anyway, if Oswain thinks so.'

'I just hope you're right, that's all I can say.'

And so they continued, until they came in sight of the castle. With hearts thumping rather loudly, they began to walk in full view towards the dark and forbidding main door. Dead bats hung from trees on either side of them which made the mice shiver with disgust. Just as they came under the castle's shadow a Grog guard stepped out to bar their way with his spear.

'Halt! What's yer business 'ere? Don't yer know yer trespassin'? Yer can git yer froat cut fer that.' He grinned wickedly, showing his broken yellow teeth, and brandished his spear in their faces.

'Please, sir, your honour,' began Fumble. 'We have come to beg an audience with the great Queen Hagbane. We bring an important message for her and we come in peace.'

At this point Grumble produced a white flag and waved it before the guard.

'News, eh? And yer want ter see 'er majesty do yer? Wait 'ere, vermin, an' I'll go an' ask 'er if she wants ter see yer. An' if she don't, I'll slit yer froats,' he added as an afterthought before vanishing inside.

'Do you think it's going to work?' whispered Grumble.

'I hope so. Anyway so far so good. Look out, here she comes!'

The witch appeared before them and fixed them with a baleful glare.

'You! Yes, I've seen you before, haven't I? With those meddling children, were you not? And you have thwarted me twice. Fools,' she screamed. 'For that you shall die—and very slowly.'

The mice trembled before her evil presence but

somehow managed to keep their nerve.

'But, please, your majesty,' said Fumble. 'Before you kill us, please hear what we have come to say. We have come in peace with a message from the forest-folk.'

'Message? What message? Speak, vermin scum. Your life depends on whether I like what I hear.' She advanced menancingly towards the hapless mouse.

'If it pleases you, your highness, mighty queen of the Great Forest, we deeply regret the fighting which has gone on between us over the years and we would dearly like to put matters to rights with you. Your dreadful power, your fearsome might are never to be forgotten. Your majesty, the people of the Forest crave an audience with you in the forest to show you how they really feel about you.'

The witch glared suspiciously at the mouse but then, as Trotter had correctly surmised, her vanity got the better of her. She interpreted the speech as praise.

'Really?' Her eyes gleamed. 'So you have seen sense at last, have you?'

'I believe we have, your majesty,' replied Fumble solemnly.

'Very well, I shall grant you your request. Where shall it be?'

'If it please your highness, we would like for you to come to the old clearing at noon today. It is an ancient place of honour, fitting for such an occasion,' the mouse replied.

'And you will demonstrate your loyalty to me?'

'Your majesty, we will be prepared to demonstrate all we owe you.'

'Then this is how I shall want it shown. You will hand over those children of men to me. Do you understand? They do not belong to the Forest and I must deal with them. Is that clear?'

'B..b..but, your majesty...'

'Silence! You speak of owing me something. Very well, we shall soon see!'

'If you say so, ma'am,' said Grumble.

'I shall bring my guards too. So no tricks,' she threatened. 'And if you fail, I shall take my vengeance upon you all. I shall show no mercy.'

'We understand, your majesty.'

'Then go, before I lose patience with you. No, wait. You!' she pointed at Fumble. 'You almost questioned my will. I shall keep you as a gesture of good faith. If you are deceiving me, you shall be the first to die. Guard, take him!'

Before the others could protest, Fumble was marched firmly away to the dungeons, followed by Hagbane. Which left Mumble and Grumble with nothing else to do except return to the Forest.

'Hmmmm, that didn't work out too well. Poor old Fumble. I didn't expect that,' said Grumble. 'I hope he'll be all right.'

'Ocorsewildonwori,' said Mumble.

'What? Oh, never mind. Well all I can say is, it's *got* to work, for Fumble's sake,' he spoke fiercely. 'Come on, we'd better report back to the others. Goodness knows how they're going to sort all this out.'

Chapter Eleven

HAGBANE TRIPS UP

The old clearing, as it was known, was an open grassy area surrounded by gorse bushes, about one kilometre from Hagbane's castle. For many years it had been used as a meeting place where the forest-folk and their leaders gathered for public discussions but, since Hagbane had come to power, nobody had met there. It was quite close to her castle and, in any case, such meetings were forbidden under her rule.

Thus it was with some trepidation that the forest-folk gathered together in the clearing. In fact, many would have preferred not to have come and it was only the combined efforts of Trotter and Aldred which finally persuaded them. Terrifying though she was, the image which most animals had of Hagbane was far worse than the truth; something she was not slow to exploit. It is strange how folk are apt to make either too little of evil and so do nothing to check it or to make too much of it and so lose the courage necessary to halt its progress. Either way, evil prospers. Only those who respect the power of evil and yet believe firmly in the greater power of goodness can hope to triumph.

Such a one was Trotter who stood alone and unafraid at the head of an uneasy gathering of animals in that ancient clearing. A weak sun filtered through the silvery-grey sky, giving small comfort as the hour of meeting drew near. All was silent until Aldred called out that the witch was on her way with a large company of Grogs. Each animal nervously checked his position and waited. Soon they could see the gaunt, black shape striding towards them, hair and cloak swirling, with the gang of Grogs marching raggedly behind her.

High in the sky Arca hovered between the clearing and the sun, so as not to be seen. From his back Sarah looked down on the Forest. She could make out the dark specks of the animals against the greenness of the grass. She could see the castle and the paths which led from it. Then she saw Hagbane and her Grogs making their way to the clearing.

'Now is our chance,' cawed Arca, who saw it all much better, of course. 'But we must be in haste for there will be little time to lose.'

So saying, he soared in a wide sweeping arc and then swooped low over the tree tops, out of Hagbane's line of vision, and over the castle walls. Sarah prepared to use the mirror. Moments later they landed and almost immediately were rushed by the few remaining guards. Gilmere shot forth its light, striking one Grog after another, how many Sarah never knew. And as before, each became a frightened frog fleeing for its life. The opposition had been almost insignificant.

'So far so good,' panted Sarah, closing the mirror 'Now what?'

Glancing around the courtyard they immediately spied many iron-barred gates from which all sorts of animals stared wide-eyed.

'Don't be alarmed,' called Sarah. 'We've come to rescue you.'

She ran from gate to gate, training the mirror on the locks. In an instant they flew open and freedom lay before the captive animals. Many could hardly believe it and walked out stunned; others leapt out joyfully and danced about the courtyard; some who were very weak had to be carried from their cells. However, soon a great crowd of stoats, foxes, weasels, squirrels, moles, voles and badgers was assembled. Sarah, meanwhile, had run downstairs to the basement cells where Peter had been held. There she found many more animals and busied herself releasing them. It was here too that she found Fumble who was so overjoyed to see her that he flung himself against her and brought them both crashing to the ground in fits of laughter.

Arca, meanwhile, organized an air-lift over the walls for the weakest of the animals so that they could escape into the seclusion of the trees as soon as possible. At length, Sarah came panting up the stairs followed by a jubilant host of creatures. She ran across to the main gate and trained Gilmere's light on to the lock, muttering a prayer to Elmesh that it would work. Slowly, the great oak doors swung back. It was then that misfortune struck them. Even as the gates opened a loud, raucous trumpeting sounded from high on the wall.

'It must be some kind of alarm,' gasped Sarah in dismay. 'Quick, all of you, run for it! Run for your lives!'

.   .   *   .   .

Hagbane strode purposefully into the clearing. She stopped before the assembled animals, folded her arms and fixed them with an imperious gaze. Her guards halted a little distance behind.

'Well?' she demanded. 'Here I am, your queen! Do you have someone who can speak?'

She deliberately overlooked Trotter. However, the old badger was not to be outdone.

'Yes, your majesty, as lore-master of the forest-folk, I will address you.' He spoke boldly and with dignity.

Hagbane frowned in annoyance. 'Very well, speak on, whatever you call yourself. I do not recognize positions *I* have not appointed, but just this once, I will listen to you. So speak, and make it good—or I'll make it bad.' She cackled at her own wit.

Trotter unfurled a scroll and cleared his throat.

'Ahem. If it please your majesty I, Trotter, offspring of Rufus the Strong, member of the Forest elders of the old days, I who am appointed lore-master of the forest-folk by Elmesh's command, address you on a matter of great importance. For long years, your majesty, you have held power in this Forest by virtue of your possessing the Merestone. Many of us have fought against you these years and there has been much suffering for our people, many deaths, many imprisonments. The Forest has grown weary and is dying. The time has come for this to end, your majesty; the days of war must cease and peace return to the Great Forest. We would like to express some feelings of loyalty *if* we could—but first you must show your true queenliness before us, not by violence but by returning the Merestone to its rightful place and....'

'What is this insolent nonsense?' Hagbane had been growing increasingly irritated by Trotter's speech. Now she could contain herself no longer. 'How dare you speak to me like this, you impudent filth! Trying to tell me what to do? Me? Hagbane, the mighty queen of all this land! You bring me out for *this*? I will have no more of it.' Her voice was hard and angry, cold as steel. She spoke through gritted teeth. 'But I will have your loyalty. Bring me those children. Bring them at once before I destroy you all.'

Trotter had known all along that he would have little time but had hoped to delay the witch as long as possible. He tried to stall her.

'I am sorry my words displease you, your majesty. Please accept my....'

'Enough! Where are the children of men?'

'I..er..they are not actually quite here, if you see what I mean.'

'No I do not. Bring them this instant.'

'But, your majesty....'

At that moment, he was interrupted by a loud trumpeting sound which echoed across the Forest. It clearly came from the direction of her castle.

'Stop!' Hagbane cried out. Her face contorted with rage. 'I've been tricked. Tricked! Do you hear that? It's the alarm.'

She turned to her guards, fists clenched, brows thunderous with fury.

'Kill them! Kill every one of them. I want no mercy. Tear them limb from limb,' she screamed. 'And you can start with him.'

The old crone turned and pointed at Trotter. Only Trotter was not there. Nor indeed were any of the other animals. Everyone had vanished as though into thin air. Hagbane looked around her, eyes popping with amazement.

'What's the meaning of this? What trickery is going on?' she spoke threateningly—even though no one was there to hear.

Angrily, she stepped forward and, the next moment, fell flat on her face. Her foot had caught itself in a deep hole barely covered by grass. For a moment she just lay there and then she arose and slowly realization dawned as she saw the size and depth of the hole.

'So, this is how they escaped, is it?'

'There's another one 'ere, yer 'ighness,' called a Grog. 'And another.'

'And another. The place is full of holes.'

'It's a plot,' the witch screamed. She jumped up and down in a frightful rage, cursing everything she could think of. 'Why? What are they up to? I'll make them pay for this.'

The holes were too small for her guards to go down and so all they could do was run around searching in the gorse. But that was quite futile.

'Come here, you fools,' the witch called. 'Back to the castle. Run! Something's up and I don't like it.'

So saying, she gathered up her skirts and ran after her guards as fast as her legs could carry her.

Deep in the Forest Peter puffed as he spoke.

'Phew, that was close. I thought Trotter had misjudged it for a moment.'

'Yes,' Oswain agreed. 'But it worked. A brilliant idea of Stiggle's, even if it was risky.'

'What was the trumpet sound?' Andrew queried.

'I think it must have been an alarm of some kind,' Oswain said. 'Let us go and see if they are all right. Although I do not really have any fears where Arca is concerned.'

What had in fact taken place was the result of a careful plan which had begun the night before with dozens of animals, especially moles and rabbits, digging long tunnels from behind the gorse bushes into the centre of the old clearing. From these long tunnels came shorter ones, and from these, shorter ones still until the whole area had a subterranean lattice work of tunnels. Then many holes to the surface had been made and carefully covered with grass. When the animals had assembled the next day, each one had stood just in front of a hole or as near as possible (some had shared one). The moment Hagbane turned to address her guards, at a signal from Trotter, they had simply stepped backwards and bolted into the ground.

Once in the tunnels, the forest-folk had scampered away just as fast as they could, had burst from the entrances behind the gorse and bolted into the shelter of the trees. It had been a most successful way of luring Hagbane and her guards from the castle and the animals had got away without a scratch.

Deep in the woods that afternoon there was a great converging of the forest-folk, young and old alike. This time they gathered, not in trepidation, but in great joy. It was a time of deep emotion and many tears were shed as loved ones long separated were reunited. Prisoners who had long since given up hope walked around in a daze greeting old friends and acquaintances. Parents and youngsters met again, sometimes hardly recognizing one another. Tales were exchanged of brave exploits, of courage in the face of suffering, of noble deaths. Some, whose loved ones had not returned, wept and were comforted by others. It was a most moving occasion.

'Isn't this smashing?' Andrew exclaimed. 'We've won a victory at last.'

'Yes,' Sarah replied, who was weeping a bit herself. 'Yes, it's really wonderful. I feel, well, just so happy, so full, if you know what I mean. Letting those prisoners free was the most marvellous thing that's ever happened to me. Just look at them.'

'Only just in time though,' Peter added.

Sarah nodded. 'Mmm. It was getting close. I nearly died when that alarm sounded. We didn't know what would happen, so we just ran. We'd hardly reached the trees when we saw the first of her guards running back. But we did it,' she ended triumphantly.

'Yes, you did it, and it's a happy day for us all. Elmesh be praised!' Trotter joined them, beaming through his spectacles. 'You know, I haven't seen such rejoicing in many a year, not since, well, I can't even remember.' He laughed, 'This is the first real victory we've had over that witch. She's always thwarted us before—so things are changing!'

'You were marvellous, Trotter,' Peter declared. 'I thought you were so brave to face her like that.'

'Not really, Peter. I was only doing what was necessary.'

'And that speech,' Andrew said. 'What *were* you going to say next?'

Trotter smiled modestly. 'Yes, it was a bit of a mouthful, wasn't it? But I was trying to take as long as possible, you see. If I had continued, I would have told her how evil she was and how Elmesh was angry with her. And that she had better change. That would have made her really angry. Then we would have done our vanishing trick.'

So the animals continued their rejoicing that day. Only Oswain was silent as he gazed at the joyful scene. Sarah caught the far away look in his eyes, a deep sadness, a longing, an emotion too great to be expressed. She wondered what it meant.

'Hey, look everyone!'

It was Andrew who called out and folk turned to see him pointing at the ground. Quickly, they gathered around him and stared at what he had found. There, growing proudly from the dark soil, was a bright mauve crocus, the first to be seen in many years.

'A sign of spring,' breathed Peter. 'The power of Hagbane is beginning to break.'

Chapter Twelve

OSWAIN FINDS OUT

It was very late before most of the forest-folk went to bed. The evening had been filled with laughter and tales of brave exploits. The story of the meeting in the old clearing had been told and re-told with great gusto and considerable imagination until you could be forgiven for thinking that Trotter had chased the witch away single-handed whilst the rest of the animals beat the Grogs to pulp! Others spoke of Sarah and Arca with awe and described, with many fine words, their magnificent raid on Hagbane's castle—even though the number of Grogs destroyed was somewhat exaggerated.

At length all began to quieten down and the company at Trotter's house made their weary but happy way to bed. Sleep came surprisingly easy for Sarah and for a long while she slumbered deeply. And then she began to dream.

She was floating like a feather caught in the warm upcurrent of a summer's day. Then great bats came whirling about her, swooping close with their wings flapping noisily. Sarah flinched, twisted and turned to avoid them, covering her face with her hands. She called desperately for help and was answered by the screech of Arca, hovering high above her. Flashes of white fire shot from his eyes and frizzled the bats to smoking cinders which dropped to the ground. She felt sleepy, drifting higher and higher in the balmy air, floating lazily towards the sky above.

Then in her dream she awoke with a start. She was in the witch's den where Hagbane was feeding a wild fire, cackling with glee as she did so. A bright jewel, which Sarah knew to be the Merestone, crackled with energy. Light flashed around the room and a kind of madness possessed the witch. Then, to her horror, Sarah saw Oswain being dragged into the fire by Hagbane. She started to run forward in order to save him, but however hard she ran she could get no nearer. She shouted and screamed but nobody could hear her voice. Anguish gripped her heart as the flames of the fire rose higher and higher until she could see neither the witch nor Oswain. A sheet of flame roared before her until both the heat and the noise were too much and everything went black.

She awoke, shivering with cold, not sure for a moment whether she was truly awake or still dreaming. She found she was lying on the floor with a blanket tangled around her arms and legs and her body bathed in sweat. For a while she lay there in the stillness of the night, trying to understand her dream. It was then that she heard a faint click. Curious, she arose and crept to the door. She quietly opened it just in time to see Oswain vanishing through the front door of the cottage. Sarah hesitated only for a moment before deciding to follow him.

Outside it was cool but fear and excitement made her insensitive to the cold. Stealthily, she crept from tree to tree, always keeping a good distance behind

Oswain, afraid that he might turn around suddenly and spot her. Soon she saw that he was heading for the enchanted glade.

No longer needing to worry about keeping up, Sarah followed on at a slower pace to make sure she was not seen. So she arrived at the glade a few minutes after Oswain. He was staring intently into the silvery pool whose radiance suffused his face with a soft glow, allowing Sarah to see lines of deep sadness etched into his rugged features. He shook his head slowly, his mouth forming soundless words. The powerful shoulders heaved a great sigh and his whole body shook with sorrow at what he saw. Sarah gazed wonderingly as silent tears fell from his eyes into the waiting pool, seeming themselves to catch the shimmering light of El-la before mingling with the clear water beneath. A wave of pity swept over her heart and, forgetting her secrecy, she ran across to him. Oswain lifted his head with a start but, before he could say anything, she threw her arms around him and looked up into his face beseechingly with her own tear-filled eyes.

'Please, dear Oswain, what is it? Why are you so sad?'

'Why are you here, child?' he demanded, ignoring her question. 'Did you follow me?'

'I'm sorry, but I had a terrible dream and when I woke up I heard somebody leaving. I looked out of my room and saw that it was you. So I followed you. I'm awfully sorry if I did wrong.'

He smiled tenderly at her and looked intently into her eyes so that she felt both safe and a little afraid all at once. She imagined the stars in those deep, dark eyes.

'No, you did not do wrong, Sarah. And, Elmesh knows, perhaps it is altogether right for you to be here tonight. Now tell me of your dream.'

Sarah felt reassured and they sat on a rock whilst she recounted all that she could remember. Oswain listened intently until she had finished.

'Alas, it is a true vision, Sarah, for something like this will surely come to pass. Though it is little comfort to know it beforehand.'

'What do you mean?' exclaimed Sarah. 'I don't want anything awful to happen to you. I don't understand all this.'

'No, I do not expect you to, for you have fallen into something far bigger than you have previously experienced,' he replied. 'But I will try to tell you a little.'

He arose and walked a short way from her before turning to speak.

'For long years now it has been written that I should journey to the Great Forest to undo a great evil and restore things as they were. The wise of my own country had spoken of it being the will of Elmesh and that I would be told in some way of the time to begin my journey. That happened to me in a dream not many days ago; a dream similar to yours, Sarah. In it I saw your faces and the face of Hagbane. I knew then that the hour of my destiny drew near. It was a long and difficult journey in which dark forces sought to hamper my way, but Elmesh gave me strength and I arrived as it was written. And you arrived too in a strange manner. And Arca, of course.'

'And you are to be ruler of the Forest in place of Hagbane?' Sarah asked.

'That is so,' he replied solemnly. 'It is Elmesh's

decree.'

'Then why are you so sad? I don't understand. After all, we have already begun to defeat her. Yet you were sad this afternoon and now you have seen something in the pool which has made you even more unhappy.'

He nodded.

'I knew when I set out that there would be suffering and pain. I did not fear that, for even though I did not understand all that was to come to pass, I trusted that Elmesh would keep me. Yet I could not see why I should be chosen for this destiny. Even the sages of my father's household could not tell me that.'

'And is that what you have discovered tonight?' whispered Sarah.

Oswain was silent for a moment, struggling with something inside himself.

'Yes,' he spoke with great effort. 'Tonight, the pool has spoken and told me why it is I and I alone who must walk this path—and I am saddened by the knowledge.'

He turned and walked away. Sarah ran after him and pulled at his sleeve.

'Oswain, why? What is it?' she pleaded. 'Please tell me!'

He hesitated and gazed into her earnest face. Almost he spoke but nothing came.

'I am sorry, Sarah,' he answered at length. 'But I cannot speak it. It is too much for me and I must think.'

'Oh, Oswain, this is too terrible. What ever must it be? And my dream. Oh . . . my dream! Does it mean you will die?'

He was silent and Sarah felt quite helpless. She began to sob.

'No...no...please don't let it be so. There must be another way.'

He put his hands on her shoulders and spoke quietly.

'Sarah, it is the will of Elmesh.'

She nodded.

'But is there nothing we can do? Is there no other way? Oh, why does it have to be like this?'

He shook his head slowly.

'You ask questions too deep for you to understand the answers. You must await the outcome—and there may yet be some surprises. After all, you and your brothers have a part to play.'

'Fat lot of use we've been,' sniffed Sarah. 'All we've done is get in the way so far.'

'That is not true,' he reassured her. 'Tonight you have done a precious thing. You have brought me comfort in the loneliness of my destiny. I shall not forget that. Now come, we must depart before daylight. And please, not a word of this to anyone.'

She nodded and put her arm around him as best she could.

'Look, up there. See how bright El-la shines tonight.'

And then warm hope filled their souls and they were at peace. They returned swiftly to Trotter's house where they found that they had not been missed. Sarah slept soundly for the rest of the night.

.   .   *   .   .

But another was not sleeping. Hagbane burned with fury. Her initial discovery of the loss of her prisoners had sent her into a rage of such intensity that her guards fled before her and cowered in the now empty dungeons. All the rest of that day she stormed, screeching out her hatred and vowing terrible destruction upon her enemies.

At length, her energies spent, she lapsed into gloomy silence for the rest of the evening and slowly her troops crept about their business, not daring to disturb her. For long hours she neither ate nor drank as she brooded in self-pity.

And then her mood changed. The anger returned but this time it was not an explosive rage but a cold, calculating fury which possessed her. Her eyes gleamed with hatred as she thought about the forest-folk.

'I shall destroy them all this time,' she muttered. 'I shall show no mercy. I've been far too soft on them. But not any longer! Every one of them shall die and I shall extend my power till I conquer the world. No one will ever make a fool of me like this again. How dare they think they can do this to me and get away with it? To me! Hagbane the mighty!'

She rose and began to pile strange powders and repulsive objects together on her table. Swiftly, she moved to and fro, glancing from time to time at books of magic and all the while muttering threats against her foes. At last the foul mixture was complete and she placed it in an iron bowl on a tripod in the middle of the room. She pointed her wand beneath it and, in an instant, a fire began to burn, heating the contents of the bowl.

Hagbane watched as the mixture began to simmer. Her evil eyes glowed yellow in the firelight and dark shadows flickered about the room. Satisfied, she went to the corner and carefully fetched the Merestone which she placed, still covered, on a stool on the other side of the tripod. Almost with reverence she lifted the cloth cover. The jewel glowed dully with its own hidden fire. Hagbane chuckled.

'Now we shall see what we shall see.'

She sat down opposite the tripod so that the simmering mixture was between herself and the Merestone. An empty blackness descended upon the room. The witch began to sway gently to and fro and a low moan escaped her lips. She commenced an incantation, eyes closed and her body swaying in rhythm. Louder and louder she chanted, her voice gaining in intensity. A blue flame began to hiss above the iron bowl, lighting her evil features with a ghostly hue. Her eyes opened, unseeing, and she seemed as one of the undead. The flame hissed higher and an icy wind filled the air. Doors slammed and things clattered. The room seemed to tilt. Formless shapes whirled about the witch and soldiers cowered in nameless dread as she summoned the forces of darkness to her aid.

The wind rose to a desolate howl, the room shook and the Merestone flashed a terrible flame which shattered the tripod and its contents. Hagbane fell and lay silent.

For a long time she lay, unmoving, and then slowly she rose to her hands and knees. A gleam came into her eye and a leer twisted her mouth as she saw what lay before her. There, in the ruins of the tripod, lay a grey rod, about a forearm's length and as thick as a broomstick, pointed at each end. Hagbane stretched out a scrawny hand and grasped it. The rod tingled to the touch, possessed of some strange and terrible power. She clutched it greedily to her bosom.

'Heh, heh,' she breathed, a mad look in her eyes. 'I've done it. With this sceptre I shall rule the world. All power shall be mine. All shall despair before me!'

Chapter Thirteen

WHAT SORDA OVERHEARD

The next morning saw the Forest alive with activity. Sober common sense returned after the rejoicing and boastings of the previous night. It would surely not be long before the thwarted witch sought vengeance on the forest-folk. So it was that many began to make preparations, especially those who lived close to her castle. In fact, quite a number decided to move house and made their way to the vicinity of the enchanted glade. Others dug deep burrows and moved their meagre food supplies and scanty possessions as far underground as possible.

'Aren't you going to move house too, Trotter?' asked Peter.

'Not me,' the old badger replied. 'I have lived too long in this place to leave it now. And Mrs Trotter would never dream of doing so, in any case. No, we shall stay and leave our fate in Elmesh's hands.'

'All the same,' Andrew interrupted. 'You ought to have some protection at least. After all, you are the one she's most likely to be after.'

'Well,' smiled Trotter. 'I've got Aldred and Stiggle. They're afraid of very little, you know.'

'Yes, but....'

'Trotter is right.' The speaker was Oswain, who had just entered the room. 'This moving is, I think, unnecessary; for I sense that things will not go as many of the forest-folk are fearing. The days of Hagbane are now numbered.'

'What do you mean?' Andrew asked. 'Can't you tell us what's going to happen? We know you told Sarah some things last night but she won't say anything.' He gave a sidelong glance at Peter. 'After all, we're part of this, too, and I think we have a right to know what's going on.'

'You went to the Star Pool in the night?' Trotter asked. 'And did you find out your destiny?'

Oswain nodded, his face betraying just a flicker of emotion.

'Let's talk outside,' he said. 'It's rather close in here and the sun is shining this morning. You are quite right, Andrew. I do owe it to you to tell you more of what is happening.'

And so Trotter, the children, Aldred and Stiggle, found a grassy bank and sat down to hear what Oswain had to say.

'Long ago,' he began, 'as far back in the mists of time as you can imagine, the Great Forest was appointed by Elmesh to be a very special place. Somehow it was given a certain magic. Indeed, there are those who say that Elmesh himself walked these paths and it was his presence which enchanted this Forest. Certainly the glade, which has been untouched by Hagbane's curse, retains its enchantment.'

The others nodded their agreement.

'Legend has it,' Oswain continued, 'that a small meteorite from El-la plunged into the Forest and its impact carved out the pool. That is why it is called

Elmere, the Star Pool.'

'And that is why there remains a kinship between the starlight and the water. I too have heard of the meteorite. Some say it is the origin of the Merestone,' added Trotter.

'Then it's from outer space,' cried Andrew excitedly.

'If that is what it should be called,' replied Oswain. 'One day you may find it is less "outer" than you imagine. But be that as it may. Certainly, the Merestone is no ordinary jewel, for it possesses a power of its own and while it lay in the enchanted glade it exercised a benign influence over the whole of the Great Forest. The trees which you can see around you grew tall and fair and birds of every kind and colour rested in their branches. Flowers bloomed in colours and scents which could take your breath away. But, Trotter, you know more of this for you lived in the latter end of those days.'

The badger nodded. 'Yes, they were wonderful times indeed and I remember them well. I should say that it was in those days, before there was any trouble, that Gilmere was formed in the pool and the prophecies were delivered by the wise. Strange that.'

'And then Hagbane came?' Peter asked.

'Yes, but before that there was a day when some deep violence occurred throughout all creation. A violence which shook the very heavens themselves,' said Oswain. 'A grim foreboding fell upon all peoples. In the Wester Lands, where I come from, there was much fear and unrest. It seemed that people were always on the move but didn't know where they were going. Bands of outlaws began to appear around our towns and many evil deeds were committed. It was as though we had lost control of our lives. Even the air we breathed seemed somehow threatening.'

'Here, in the Forest, nothing changed because of its special enchantment. That is, until one dark night.' He hesitated. 'One day a woman appeared from outside the Forest. She came as a pilgrim to Elmere. The woman was young, and fair to look upon, but a bitter evil had already poisoned her heart. She gazed upon the Merestone and greed demanded that she possess it.'

'Hagbane!' they breathed in unison.

He nodded sadly.

Sarah regarded him curiously.

'She came from your country, didn't she? And....'

'Yes,' he cut in before she could continue, 'and on a certain night she entered the glade again and, by some terrible magic, wrested the Merestone from the Star Pool. Clutching her glittering prize, she fled from the Forest back to her own land. From that moment the Great Forest began to die. The trees shed their leaves. Birds perished or fled. Flowers drooped, never to rise again.'

'For a little while we could not understand what was happening,' continued Trotter, 'until it was reported that the Merestone had vanished. Despair filled our hearts, for we did not know what had become of the jewel. All we heard was a rumour of a woman visiting the glade some time before. It was not until a year later that the full and awful truth dawned upon us.'

'Was that when Hagbane returned?' asked Andrew.

'Yes,' said Oswain. 'She came with Grogs and Grims, evil creatures which she herself had had a part in producing. She erected her castle and began cruelly to dominate the forest-folk. Many died who tried to oppose her and many were taken captive, to be used in her evil experiments.'

'The wicked witch! How I hate her!' exclaimed Sarah angrily.

Oswain held up his hand.

'All was not lost, however. The enchanted glade closed itself off from Hagbane so that she has not been able to find it to this day. Whenever she tries, she loses her direction and comes back to where she started. And that is why the glade preserves something of the former life of the Forest. Only those who are unpolluted by her evil may venture there. The wise, such as Trotter and his father before him, learned to seek wisdom at Elmere and to discern the voice of Elmesh. Which is why Trotter knew of your coming.'

'When my father was dying,' said Trotter, 'he passed on to me Gilmere and the prophecy which I showed to you when you first came here. For long years I waited and listened until I knew the time of deliverance was at hand.'

'And that's when we walked in?' Peter asked.

'Yes, and then Oswain himself. The ruler who was promised from of old.'

'Where did you get your ring?' Andrew enquired.

'It came from my mother,' he answered. 'The stone which you see is part of the Merestone itself. You see, I discovered last night when I looked into the Star Pool that she had obtained it as the outcome of a desperate bid to wrest the Merestone from Hagbane.'

They gasped at this news.

'Then your mother has met Hagbane?' demanded Stiggle.

Oswain was experiencing some difficulty in speaking.

'More than that,' he replied slowly. 'I also have

known Hagbane before.'

There was a stunned silence at this news. Then everyone gabbled at once.

'Who is she, Oswain?'

'How do you know her?'

'Where did you meet her?'

Before Oswain could respond to the barrage of questions, there was a sharp crack as a twig snapped in the bushes behind them.

Aldred held up his paw.

'Quiet everyone,' he urged. 'There's somebody there, I think.'

Everyone leapt to their feet, tense and alert. They stared at the unmoving shrubs. Slowly, with Stiggle leading in one direction and Aldred in the other, they encircled the bushes. Then, hearts thumping, they rushed in from both sides, only to find that there was nobody to be seen.

'Perhaps we were imagining it,' said Peter.

'I don't think so,' Aldred replied, pointing at a broken twig. 'Look, it's not safe to talk for too long outside like this. We should have been more sensible and set a guard. Spies are nothing new to the Forest.'

'Yes, yes, you are quite right, Aldred,' agreed Trotter. 'We must warn everyone to be alert to the dangers. In fact, we should do that right away. I just hope not too much was overheard, if anyone was listening.'

The sun passed behind a cloud and it was suddenly chilly. They shivered and nodded.

'Let's set out in pairs and pass the message around,' suggested Stiggle.

Everyone agreed and set off to do this. Nobody, for the moment, remembered the unanswered questions, except Sarah, who thought that she knew.

.   .   *   .   .

Not far away, a beady-eyed Sorda watched with an oily smile on his round face.

'Very interesting,' he said to himself. 'Very interesting indeed!'

The wily wizard had overheard every word of the conversation and already his scheming mind was hard at work. Glancing about him quickly, he hurried back to Terras in their underground lair.

The other wizard was hardly in a good mood when Sorda arrived. He was still trying to put together what was left out of the mess created by the children's onslaught three days before. Not only that, but they had been on the receiving end of Hagbane's wrath for having failed to provide a sacrifice for her Grims. She had quite refused to listen to their explanations and warned them that if they did not improve quickly they had better leave the Forest or die. The news of Hagbane's recent defeats only made them more afraid of displeasing her.

'Where on earth have you been?' snapped Terras. 'Can't you see there's work to be done? Here am I working my fingers to the bone and all you can do is wander off. I thought we were supposed to be partners. What do you think she's going to say if we don't start up again soon? Eh?'

'Far from doing nothing, I've been finding out things of great value to us,' the other replied.

'Here, give me a hand with this table, will you? Or at least, what's left of it. If only I could get my hands on those children again—and those mice. What've you been finding out, anyway?'

'Stop messing about with all this and I'll tell you. By the time we've finished, my friend, we shall have our own suite of rooms in the castle itself. Now listen.'

Sorda recounted all that he had seen and heard. When he had finished, Terras's eyes gleamed. He rubbed his bony fingers together gleefully.

'Heh, heh. Not only will this get us back into her good books, but it'll also destroy those children. Play this one right and we've got it made.'

'Just think, a proper spell-room and real power. Perhaps even the use of the Merestone.' Sorda's eyes glittered at the thought.

'We must go to Hagbane tonight and share our news. I'm sure she will be most interested to hear what we've found out.'

'What *I've* found out,' corrected Sorda.

.   .   *   .   .

That night dark counsels took place in Hagbane's lair. The air hung heavily, thick with evil, as the trio plotted the doom of Oswain and the children.

Hagbane had received the two wizards impatiently at first and kept them standing while they spoke. But, at the mention of Oswain's name her attitude changed. She sat them down, eager to know more.

'Oswain. Oswain.' A strange look passed across her eyes as she mouthed the name. 'So it's him, is it? And after all these years.'

'They spoke about prophecies,' said Sorda. 'Something about him being a ruler.'

'Pah,' replied the witch. 'The prophecies are the vain hopes of fools. Don't you know that I hold the Meréstone and nobody can defeat me? Nobody, do you hear?'

'Yes, your highness,' replied Terras hastily.

The truth was that Hagbane had been disturbed by the mention of Oswain's name. Although she did not accept the prophecies, she did respect the fact that both he and the children had come as predicted. The only way to deal with her unease was to act as soon as possible, but wisely. To achieve her ends she was quite prepared to form an alliance with the wizards. They could be dealt with at a later date.

'We must work together,' she cackled. 'This Oswain must be destroyed somehow and I want to do it myself. None of us is safe while he lives, do you understand?'

They nodded.

'Good. Then we will set a trap between us and lure them all to their doom. This is what I suggest....'

Evil hands clasped one another as the plot hatched. Three pairs of eyes gleamed in the darkness. Hagbane thought of a new use to which she could put her newly-forged weapon and smiled as she pictured the scene in her mind. An old score would be settled at last and the day of her vengeance was fast approaching.

Chapter Fourteen

THE TRAP IS SPRUNG

Since the warning had been given everyone in the Forest walked warily with their eyes and ears open for spies who might be lurking in the undergrowth. This was becoming more difficult for a very exciting reason —life was beginning to return to the Great Forest. Buds were swelling and leaves had started to unfold. The lone crocus had been the herald of many others and new patches of bright colour startled the eye. Some new, more powerful magic was at work. But thicker foliage created problems when it came to watching out for spies, for camouflage was that much easier.

Still more of the forest-folk moved closer to the enchanted glade. Hagbane had been ominously quiet for the past three days and tension ran high amongst the animals. Flashes of light had been seen coming from the castle at night and black smoke by day. Something was going on.

The company in Trotter's home could only sit and wait for the next move, for clearly there was little they could do. Oswain seemed unwilling to continue his interrupted explanations and was in a brooding mood which not even Sarah dared to intrude upon. By the third day everyone was getting just a bit irritable. They were tired of being cooped up indoors. On that day Trotter and Aldred ventured out early in the morning to attend to various matters amongst the forest-folk.

'I'm fed up with this!' exclaimed Peter. 'I'll go round the bend if we have to sit here much longer.'

'Well, what shall we do?' asked Sarah.

'I don't know, but I must get out of this house. Anyone want to come for a walk?'

'Yes, let's do that,' said Andrew. 'I'm fed up with being stuck here, too.'

'Just mind you're careful, my dears,' said Mrs Trotter, who had overheard them. 'And don't be too long now.'

'Thank you Mrs T. We'll watch out, don't you worry. And we've got Gilmere with us in any case.'

The weather was beautiful outside, bright, fresh and clear. The children breathed deeply.

'It does smell good, doesn't it?' Sarah said. 'There's less of that dead smell than when we first arrived. Which way shall we go?'

'Let's follow this path to the left,' Andrew suggested.

And so the children enjoyed a pleasant stroll down the meandering woodland path and were soon feeling much happier. They had been walking for about twenty minutes when, all of a sudden, there was a movement in the bushes bordering the path just ahead. They all froze as, the next instant, none other than Sorda the wizard stepped out in front of them. Sarah stifled a scream and Peter's hand dived into his pocket for the mirror. He was about to open it when Sorda spoke, smooth and soft.

'I wouldn't do that if I were you, young man. At

least, not if you wish to see your friend Trotter alive and well again.'

'What do you mean?' Peter demanded. 'What have you done with him?'

'Not me. I haven't touched him,' Sorda sneered. 'No, Hagbane has. Or rather her Grogs. They've caught him.'

'Oh, no!' gasped Sarah. 'Not our dear Trotter. Oh, what shall we do?'

'Rescue him, of course,' snapped Peter, rather more sharply than he had intended. 'That is, if he's really been captured.' He spoke to the wizard. 'Why are you telling us this? After all, you're an ally of Hagbane and you tried to kill us. What sort of trap is this?'

Sorda smiled back.

'What's in it for me? Why, I'm changing sides, that's what. I want to bring Hagbane down, the same as you. And you have the power.' He indicated Gilmere.

'We don't make bargains with the likes of you,' Peter replied. 'So you can forget it. We're not interested.'

'You overlook the fact that Trotter is caught and not far from here. They'll be taking him to her and you know what that'll mean. And I know where you can stop them.'

'I don't believe you,' Peter replied.

'Hey, listen, Pete. I'm not sure I believe him either, but we've got to take a chance, just in case. It would be awful if Trotter really is caught.'

'Yes, Peter, please let's check it, just to be sure.'

Peter hesitated before addressing the wizard again.

'You'll have to prove yourself to us. Take us to Trotter and, if he's rescued, we'll think about what you've said. If you try anything funny I'll fry you alive. Now move!' he gestured angrily with the mirror.

Sorda flinched and, muttering to himself, stumbled down the path in front of them. He seemed to be taking Peter's threat seriously and kept glancing nervously over his shoulder as he hurried along.

'Just keep your eyes open for a trap,' hissed Andrew. 'This path is leading us towards the old clearing, I reckon.'

'Well, we'll know soon enough if he's telling the truth, we're nearly there,' Peter muttered.

Just as he spoke, Sorda gave a cry of fright and, to their astonishment, fell crashing into a hole in the path and disappeared from their sight. The children stopped in their tracks.

'He's fallen into a trap!' exclaimed Andrew.

'Do you think it was meant for us?'

But before anyone could answer her question, all three were thrown to the ground by the weight of a huge net which was dropped on them from the trees above. Six Grogs leapt to the ground and swiftly bundled up the children, whose struggles only entangled them further. To his dismay, Peter realized that he had dropped the mirror in the confusion. The Grogs thrust a pole through the mesh, and, balancing it on their shoulders, carried the children rapidly into the clearing ahead. They were followed by a grinning Sorda who was brushing down his clothes, having climbed out of the pit. Sarah looked back and saw his smirk.

'That wicked wizard. It was a trap after all. I'm so sorry, Pete. It's my fault for saying we should go with him.'

'No, it's mine too,' said Andrew.

'Nobody's to blame,' Peter replied. 'Let's just hope they haven't got Trotter as well. If only I hadn't dropped Gilmere....'

The Grogs came to a halt and stood to attention in the clearing. Their captives watched helplessly as the waiting Hagbane slowly approached them.

'Heh, heh, heh! Stupid young fools. You fell right into my trap. Heh, heh, heh! I've caught you good and proper this time, haven't I?'

'You're evil and horrible and nasty! I hate you!' cried Sarah. 'Let us go. Just let me get at you, you wicked witch!'

She struggled violently in the net.

'That's right, my dear, get it out of your system,' the witch replied. 'Your words mean nothing to me and it's too late for you to interfere with my plans now, in any case. Guards, prepare the next part of the plan. You know what to do.'

At her command, the Grogs carried their struggling load across the clearing until they came to a pole shaped like an old-fashioned hangman's post. There they dropped the children in a heap and fixed a rope to the net which they then threw over the cross-bar. With much puffing, the Grogs hauled on the rope until the children were suspended in the net about two metres off the ground. They struggled to readjust themselves.

'What are they doing?' gasped Andrew.

'I don't know,' his brother replied. 'I thought for one moment that we were going to be hanged.'

'I'm frightened,' Sarah whimpered. 'I don't like this at all. If only Oswain were here. Oh, what's going to happen next?'

As if in answer to their questions the guards returned to them carrying bundles of dried gorse from the bushes surrounding the clearing. For a moment they couldn't understand what was happening. The Grogs began to pile the gorse beneath the children.

'Is she going to drop us into it?' whispered Andrew. 'It looks ever so prickly.'

'No, I don't think so,' Peter muttered grimly, as the truth slowly dawned on him. Sarah also caught on to what was happening.

'She's going to burn us alive, I know it!' She shrieked.

Her dreams came rushing back with stark vividness. She screamed with all her might.

The three children stared, horror-struck, as Hagbane advanced on them bearing a burning brand in her hand. Her face twisted into an evil leer. Slowly, a bass drum began to beat. Two Grogs put trumpets to their lips and began to blow long raucous blasts. Vainly the children struggled as the witch drew close.

.   .   *   .   .

In the depths of the Forest everyone heard the beat of the drum and the blare of the trumpet. They stopped what they were doing and began to ask one another what was going on. Trotter and Oswain were together when it began.

'Something is happening,' said Trotter.

'Yes, we had better investigate. I suspect it is Hagbane making her move at last,' Oswain replied.

'I wonder where the children have got to? I haven't seen them for quite some time.'

'Nor have I, and I don't like it. Come on, Trotter, that sound is coming from the direction of the old clearing if I'm not mistaken. Come on, hurry!' Oswain sounded grim.

They raced out of the house together and found themselves along with many other of the forest-folk rushing towards the incessant beat of the drum and the insistent blast of the trumpet. It took some time to reach the clearing and they were quite puffed out when they arrived.

As they drew near, everyone quietened down and proceeded cautiously, creeping through the thick gorse. The sight that met their eyes stunned them. There were the children hanging helplessly from the post and Hagbane before them clutching her burning torch. Dozens of Grogs stood to attention in a semi-circle behind them. The sound of the instruments continued monotonously.

'They've caught the children,' gasped Trotter.

'Yes, I was afraid of that,' Oswain replied. 'So this is how it is going to happen.' He spoke almost to himself.

'Surely she's not going to kill them,' cried the badger. 'I must try to stop her.'

He darted forward, heedless of his age or personal danger. Fearlessly, he approached the witch.

'Ha, so you've arrived, have you?' she snapped, glaring venomously at him. 'All of you I trust?' She emphasized the 'all'.

'Trotter, go back! Don't worry about us. Look after yourself.'

It was Sarah who shouted and the two boys joined in, entreating Trotter to return to safety.

'Take no notice of them,' snarled the witch. 'Now listen to me. I hold all the cards, so you had better....'

'No, you listen to me,' Trotter interrupted angrily. 'These children came as visitors to the Forest. They mean nothing to you. Let them go. Let them go and take me instead. They can return to their own country and you will have me as your prisoner.'

Hagbane roared with laughter.

'You! Do you think I want you, you decrepit old ruin? No, you're nothing to me. You don't seem to understand, you old fool, I am playing for higher stakes. You have one with you, a man, Oswain. It is him I want. I want him delivered bound to me, do you understand?'

'No, no,' called the children. 'Don't do it, Trotter. Leave us.'

'If we refuse?' the badger asked lamely, already knowing what the answer would be.

'If you refuse, I shall simply set fire to this gorse and burn your friends alive! In fact, I shall count to one hundred and if the man Oswain is not delivered bound by then, they die. Now go!'

'How can I trust you not to destroy the children anyway?'

'You can't, can you? Now hurry, I haven't got all day.'

Trotter stood for a moment, trying to think of a reply.

'One, two, three....'

He ran back to the shelter of the gorse to speak with Oswain and the others. The witch's voice rang out to the melancholy beat of the drum.

'Thirteen, fourteen, fifteen....'

'Well?' Aldred demanded when Trotter arrived. 'What does she want?'

It took Trotter just a moment to give the grim news. Aldred fumed with rage and frustration.

'She's outwitted us this time. What can we do? We lose both ways. Even a head-on charge wouldn't help now.'

'We haven't much time. We must speak with Oswain quickly.' Trotter replied. 'Where is he? Where's he got to?'

The three children hung in dread and despair. All appeared to be lost. It was them or Oswain. If only it were a dream, thought Sarah, but she knew it was happening to them for real.

'Seventy five, seventy six....' The beat went on relentlessly.

Nothing moved in the gorse. The air hung still and silent.

'Eighty nine, ninety, ninety one....'

Tension mounted to breaking point. Andrew's skin prickled.

'Ninety six, ninety seven, ninety eight....'

Hagbane moved towards the pyre with the burning brand. Implacably, she lowered it towards the gorse.

'Ninety nine, One hun....'

Chapter Fifteen

ALL SEEMS LOST

'Stop!'

The firm voice rang out across the clearing.

'It's Oswain!' cried Peter.

Hagbane looked up suspiciously and grimaced. Oswain stood tall and noble in the sunlight, in vivid contrast to the crooked old witch. He spoke again.

'Leave the children be. I agree to your terms, Hagbane; I will deliver myself up to you in exchange for their lives. See, my hands are bound.'

He began to walk towards the witch.

'Stay where you are,' she croaked. 'I want to be sure there's no trickery. You two,' she said, motioning to Terras and Sorda who had joined the Grogs, 'go and check his bonds. Hurry up now.'

The wily wizards slunk from behind the guards and made their way reluctantly across the clearing to Oswain, all the while looking about them for the signs of a trap. But there was none and Oswain stood his ground while they checked his ropes and made doubly sure of his captivity by binding another length of stout rope several times about his body, pinioning his arms to his side.

'Heh, heh, try getting out of that,' Sorda sniggered.

'It's all right,' Terras called out to Hagbane. 'He can't escape from us now.'

'Very well,' snarled the witch, hiding her relief. 'Guards, go, fetch him!'

At a signal from their captain, about half the Grogs marched towards the bound man. The children watched with glum hearts. Shouting, they knew, was no use now and the only comfort they had was that of being spared a terrible fate—at least for the moment. And so it was with silent dismay that they watched as Oswain was carried across to the witch.

Back in the gorse bushes, where the forest-folk gazed with horror, Aldred and Stiggle fumed.

'This is ridiculous! Here we are absolutely powerless while that old crone gets away with it. It makes me sick. I mean, it's stupid! She's got them all now. Why on earth did we give up Oswain as well?'

'We had no choice really, did we? He was so insistent that it was the right thing to do that we couldn't have stopped him if we'd tried. What Elmesh would wish, he said.'

'I don't know about that,' said Aldred. 'But I want action, not negotiations. I don't trust that witch as far as I can throw her. Stiggle, get the troops ready. I'm prepared to die if necessary rather than let her get away with this. Why, look, our hopes are being dashed before our very eyes. We can't sit here and just do nothing.'

Stiggled hastened to obey his captain.

The Grogs reached Hagbane with their burden and dumped Oswain on his feet before her. For a long time there was silence as the two stared at each other. At length the witch spoke.

'So. We meet again at last, Oswain, Son of the High

133

King of the West. It's been a very long time. But you have changed little by the looks of you. Just a bit older.'

Oswain continued to eye the witch sadly.

'But what has become of you, Dorinda? You have changed much since I knew you. What is this evil that has destroyed you?'

'I'm not destroyed, Oswain. Fool! Do you think outward appearance is all that matters. My beauty is my power; power which shall conquer the world. That is, when I've finished with you.' She laughed triumphantly. 'Take him away!'

'Wait! You have my life in exchange for the children. That was the agreement. Release them.'

The witch still held the flaming torch. Reluctantly she quenched it on the ground.

'Your friends can get them down. Pah!' she spat. 'I don't need them now. Not when I've got you, Oswain. No, they can go back where they came from.'

'Let him go, you rotten old witch,' Andrew shouted. 'You've no right to take him prisoner.'

The witch turned round.

'Right? Did you question my right? I hold the Merestone, fool. I have the might—so I have the right!'

Hagbane thought this sounded rather clever so she repeated it over and over again in her cackling voice as she and her guards walked back to the castle away from the despairing children.

The moment he saw that the witch and her crew were well clear of the children, Aldred spoke to Stiggle.

'It's now or never. Do you agree?'

Stiggle nodded. He glanced round at the animals assembled behind them. They were armed with just about everything they could lay their hands on. They also nodded their agreement.

'This is it then. *Charge!*' Aldred cried and led his troops at full tilt across the wide clearing. Heedless now of danger and full of pent-up fury, the animals surged towards the children and their retreating captors. They had almost reached the children when Hagbane heard the commotion behind them. She turned angrily.

'The cursed fools! Do they think to stop me now?' She screamed the question into the wind. 'Well, I'll give 'em something to think about!'

So saying, she drew her wand from beneath the folds of her gown and pointed it with cold deliberation in the direction of the captive children. A blinding flash of fire shot from its tip, bright as the sun, and the next instant the pile of gorse beneath them burst into flame.

'Meddlin' fools. That'll teach them not to tangle with me,' she snarled.

Oswain struggled vainly in his bonds as he realized what had happened.

'Put it out, Dorinda. Please,' he begged. 'They haven't harmed you. What about our bargain?'

The witch laughed with harsh indifference and Oswain groaned in defeat.

The gorse began to crackle into life as the fire took hold and smoke poured upwards, enveloping the children. Sarah screamed and the boys called hoarsely for help. Already they could feel the heat of the fire beneath them. They began to cough and splutter in the smoke and their eyes streamed.

The forest-folk, led by Aldred, stopped short in their tracks when they saw what Hagbane had done. For an instant nobody moved, each paralysed by his natural fear of fire. Then Aldred leapt forward. With no thought for his personal safety, he plunged into the burning gorse and began scattering it as far apart as possible, pushing the whole mass away from the children. The other animals reacted swiftly to their leader's example and plunged into the smoke to help. Trotter swiftly organized the remaining animals into a chain to pass along containers filled with water from a nearby stream. Vast hissing clouds of steam arose to mingle with the acrid smoke, as water was thrown on to the fire by eager helpers. Everybody was coughing and spluttering and there was much confusion as they fought to quench the blaze.

Eventually it was dealt with and the smoke began to clear. Stiggle found the rope securing the children in the net and released it. They tumbled out, shaken and exhausted and covered in soot. Their eyes stood out pink and bloodshot against the blackness of their faces as they struggled to their feet and tottered across to him.

'Oh, thank you! Thank you, Stiggle,' Peter gasped. 'I really thought we were going to die. It was terrible.'

'It's Aldred whom you must thank rather than me,' he replied. 'If it wasn't for him none of us would have had the courage to tackle this by ourselves. He just charged straight in without any thought for his own safety.'

'Yes. You're right Stiggle. But really all of you were tremendous. You saved our lives.'

'By the way, where is Aldred?' Andrew asked. 'I can't see him anywhere.'

The smoke was almost clear by now and the animals were beginning to sort themselves out. Some stood back to admire their handiwork, with satisfied smiles on their faces. Others, who had been singed here and there, were busy comparing tails and whiskers.

'Aldred? Aldred?' Peter called.

'Aldred, where are you?' cried Andrew.

There was no reply. The animals stopped their chattering and an ominous hush fell over the crowd.

'Oh!' cried Sarah. 'Oh, no! Look!'

Everyone turned to see her pointing to the ground with a trembling finger. Folk hurried across to her. There, badly burned and quite still, lay the brave Aldred. Trotter bent over him then looked up slowly, his old eyes full of tears.

'I'm afraid our noble captain is dead,' he said quietly. 'This is a terrible loss for us all.'

A stunned silence greeted this news. Then, as it sunk in, a great wail arose from the assembled forest-folk.

'He was the bravest person I ever knew,' sobbed Sarah. 'He gave his own life to save us. Oh, I can't bear it!'

She stumbled away from the dreadful scene with tears streaming down her smoke-grimed face. Great groans of anguish filled the air as all mourned this tragic loss. For a long while nobody could do anything but weep. At length, Trotter spoke gravely.

'Matters are very serious for us. Our enemy has Oswain and we have lost our fighting leader. But we must not allow ourselves to go under now. Stiggle, you must assume Aldred's role. Peter, Andrew, Sarah, we must talk swiftly. The rest of you must return home and prepare for war. This is a black day. Elmesh help us! Come, let us return to safety and bear Aldred from this awful scene.'

Four younger stoats bore away the remains of their captain upon their shoulders, walking with slow steps towards the trees and a place of burial. The stench of burnt and wet wood hung in the air and small burns began to sting in the cool wind which blew up in the last hour of that bleak afternoon. Nobody could have felt lower in spirits than the members of that sad procession winding its way into the shadows of the silent trees.

Chapter Sixteen

OSWAIN REFUSES TO BOW

'So, my dear Oswain, Son of the High King of the West; Oswain, the servant of Elmesh, at last I have you.'

Hagbane stood before her prisoner, gloating over her prize, her voice heavy with sarcasm. Oswain was bound by chains to the wall of her spellroom. He made no attempt to free himself, but gazed with mixed emotions at the witch as she rubbed her bony hands together with glee. She noticed his look.

'Can't get used to it, eh? Not like your old Dorinda, am I? What did you expect to find, eh? Some beautiful princess? Pah! You always were stupid.'

Oswain spoke with difficulty.

'I loved you, Dorinda. You were once the fairest woman in the land and the most precious person in my life. What is this evil that has overtaken you?'

'Evil? Hah! If you call power evil, then evil it is. But I desire power, Oswain. I desired it when we were young but neither you nor your family would grant it me. So I sought it for myself. And I found it,' she ended triumphantly.

'We could not give you what you wanted because you had already become evil. Pride had gripped your heart and your rule would have brought oppression upon our people if we had granted it. That is why I could not marry you, though I loved you.'

'Oh yes, you rejected me,' she spoke bitterly. 'And I have not forgotten the humiliation. I loathed you and your mother and in all these years I have cherished the day of my revenge when I should destroy you and your kin. And now you have come within my power.'

'I did not expect it to be you whom I would confront,' he replied. 'It was a deep shock when I discovered it was so in the Star Pool. I nearly turned back at that point and rejected the destiny which was chosen for me by Elmesh. The pain is a deep one, Dorinda, and I would have you give up this madness before the judgement of the prophecies falls upon you and you are destroyed. For the time of their fulfilment is at hand.'

Oswain spoke earnestly but the hag only laughed in his face.

'Yes, they say you have come to fulfil the old prophecies. Pah! I do not believe them. Delusion! Only fools listen to such old words—and you are a fool Oswain—and those meddling children. You think to scare me with vague threats? Hah! It is you who should be afraid, not I!'

He winced at the mention of the children.

'You broke your word, Dorinda, and killed them for no reason.'

'My word? Fool!' she screeched. 'You and your words. Words of prophecy. Words of honour. I care nothing for them. It is power that counts. Power, my dear Oswain, which I shall soon unleash upon the world. No brats or stupid animals shall stand in my way, and nor shall you. Your pleas are wasted. I will not change.'

'Then the vengeance of Elmesh will take place, for it is from him that you have stolen the Merestone,' replied Oswain. 'And that which you seek to use will turn against you for your own destruction.'

'I do not see why I, Hagbane, should fear Elmesh,' she retorted. 'In any case, he has hardly helped you, has he? You speak of my doom but it is yours you should fear because I have the power to do anything I want to you. The day of *my* revenge has come!'

Her wild eyes gleamed yellow as she spoke.

'Do not think these are mere words, Oswain, for I have at last created a force to make all serve me—or die! In fact,' she sniggered, 'I have planned to try it out on you. Then we shall see how worthless your prophecies are.'

So saying, she crossed to a cupboard with a dramatic swirl of her cloak, enjoying this melodrama before her captive audience. She reached in, then turned, clutching in her hand the rod which she had formed in league with the dark forces.

'With this,' she cried triumphantly. 'I shall rule the world!'

Oswain looked puzzled.

'What is it?' he asked.

'What is it? It is the power of light and darkness fused into one. It shall be terrible to behold, more powerful than even the Merestone itself, more dreadful than Grogs or Grims. By it I shall sweep all before me.'

A kind of madness filled the witch's eyes as she spoke. Oswain looked on with horror.

'Dorinda, renounce this evil while you can,' he pleaded. 'Destroy this thing lest it destroy you, I beg you.'

'Yes, you will beg, but not like this,' she answered.
'For it is not I who will change but you. You shall
become as I am and serve me or you shall die. That
will be my revenge.'

'Never!'

'We shall see. Watch!'

Hagbane pointed the rod at the floor and muttered
a spell. Oswain watched as it glowed bright orange
but did not harm her. There was a brilliant flash and a
pile of bread, loaf upon loaf, appeared before Oswain's
startled gaze. She appeared pleased and muttered
again. Another flash, and the bread frizzled to cinders.
She turned to Oswain.

'The power to create and to destroy food. I can
make plenty or I can cause famine. Who will dare
challenge me with such a temptation—or with such a
threat?'

She turned away and pointed the rod at the far wall.
Somehow Oswain could see vast multitudes of people
going about their daily business in the streets. Hagbane
muttered a spell and, to his horror, fire began to
consume one side of the picture. It grew rapidly,
devouring all before it. He heard the screams of terrified
people, saw them fleeing madly, felt the heat of the
inexorable flame as it swallowed up people and
property alike.

'Do you not think that it is a great power?' Hagbane
demanded. 'And I shall use it, make no mistake. Now
watch this.'

She held the rod at arm's length, then pointed it at
herself. Closing her eyes she cackled a spell. As Oswain
watched, still helplessly bound, she seemed to grow
larger and larger until she towered menacingly over
him. She swayed as though made of liquid and slowly

evolved into a beautiful princess who gazed upon him with dewy love-sick eyes. Oswain started as he saw again the love of his youth standing before him. He longed to reach out and touch her and his heart was filled with the yearnings of long years past. The vision again changed and she became a regal lady, cold, aloof, absolute in her power, looking down upon him with contempt. He felt the pain of utter rejection smite his heart.

The figure doubled, then trebled, quadrupled, multiplied until the room was full of Hagbanes. Their faces twisted and aged until they became nightmarishly ugly, more ugly than Hagbane herself. Terror gripped him as they advanced mercilessly towards him, long gnarled fingers outstretched like talons to tear his throat. The next moment she was a sweet little girl looking up appealingly at him and offering him an apple.

And then she was Hagbane herself. Oswain's heart jumped and his brow was covered in sweat as he sought to cope with what he had seen. He realized he was trembling.

'Impressive, eh? What do you think? There's nothing I can't do with this.'

Oswain remained silent.

'And now,' she continued. 'You will be the first to bow to me and serve me, Oswain—or you shall die.'

'I shall never bow to your evil power,' he replied, recovering his composure. 'I will no longer call you Dorinda. You are Hagbane. May Elmesh smite you!'

The witch's face darkened with fury. She screamed wildly.

'Fool, you dare to resist me? You shall worship me and plead with me before I am finished with you! You will call me your queen. I will have vengeance on you and your house.'

She stood before him with a wildness in her eyes, the years of bitterness filling her being. Slowly, she lifted the rod and pointed it with outstretched arm towards her captive. It glowed brightly in her hand and a bolt of lightning shot forth. Blue fire crackled all about him and his face contorted as one who was involved in a great struggle as the power of darkness sought to break him. He twisted and turned in his bonds but not a word passed his lips. Hagbane muttered a spell and arrows of fire pounded into Oswain's body, and still he resisted.

'Worship me,' she screeched. 'Call me your queen, curse you!'

Her hand shook with rage and the rod glowed to white heat in her grasp. Flurries of bright sparks sprayed over Oswain and he called upon Elmesh for strength. Nothing availed against him. The witch lowered the rod.

'So, you have some power after all, do you?' she muttered. 'Very well, we shall see about that. I shall break you, Oswain, or you shall perish.'

The witch crossed the room swiftly and brought forth her most prized possession, the Merestone. Carefully she placed it on a table before him.

'Now we shall see what your power is worth,' she breathed.

She removed the cover and the stone glowed with a sullen fire in the gloom. A humming noise filled the room and the jewel began to glow more brightly. Hagbane started to chant spells. The light increased and the hum became a roar.

'Acknowledge me or die now,' she screamed above

the noise. 'Even the Merestone shall obey me now, for my rod was forged in its light.'

Oswain twisted in his bonds, his face set with concentration as the power of evil sought to overwhelm him.

'Never. Never shall I bow to you, Hagbane. I reject you, by Elmesh, I refuse you.'

'Then die! Die Oswain, son of the High King,' she cried.

She pointed the rod at his chest and uttered a deep and powerful spell. The rod shone like polished silver and from the inner depths of the Merestone fire began to flash. The roar became a deafening thunder and the whole room began to shake angrily. A beam of blue light blazed forth from the Merestone and struck the ring on Oswain's finger, dissolving the gold in an instant. The sliver of the jewel it had contained flew through the air to rejoin the stone. Oswain's bonds fell from his hands and feet as Hagbane gazed in amazement. A thunderous crash marked the uniting of the Merestone and the room screamed with light.

For a moment Hagbane was stunned. Then, with a howl of rage, she lunged at Oswain with the white-hot rod. Light and fire spattered the walls, lightning flashed, the ground shook beneath their feet. With a twist of his body Oswain avoided the death-thrust and found himself locked in a desperate life and death struggle with the witch. The whole room caught fire and a mighty earthquake rent the floor upon which they fought. A wide crack opened revealing a bottomless pit from the depths of which a fire burned red. They struggled together on the brink of doom as the Merestone wreaked its own terrible revenge. Grimly they fought, oblivious to the destruction around them.

They teetered on the edge. Then Hagbane lost her footing and fell backwards into the fiery pit. Desperately she clutched at Oswain and caught him off balance. Together they fell down, down into the awesome depths of the chasm. A long piercing scream of despair echoed up from the unfathomed deeps of the flaming abyss. Fire and smoke billowed forth, filling the room until nothing else could be seen.

Chapter Seventeen

INTO BATTLE

Stiggle paced restlessly up and down in Trotter's front room, his furry face furrowed with emotion. He was deeply grieved over the loss of his commander and the all too recent burial had been difficult for him to bear. But now Trotter had made him leader of the forces; Stiggle, who had always been second-in-command; Stiggle, who was good at implementing the orders of others but who was not one to take the decisions. And his first task was to do something about Oswain! It was a worrying business.

Peter entered the room and stood for a moment watching the weasel. He sighed sympathetically.

'I know how you're feeling, Stiggle, and...well, I just want you to know that I feel the same.'

Stiggle ceased his pacing and turned to Peter.

'Thanks, my friend. It helps to know that someone understands.'

'I think we all do,' Peter replied. 'It's a terrible responsibility and it comes hard on you.'

'What do you think we should do, Peter?'

They sat down together and plunged deep into thought.

'Well, we haven't much time,' said Peter at length.

147

'If she's going to kill Oswain she'll do it quite quickly, so we must act fast. But then, he may be dead already,' he finished glumly.

'If he is or if we don't rescue him then her power will grow even more and we will be complete slaves. I'd sooner die than serve her evil ways, and I think most of our folk feel the same. I don't know about you three. You're strangers here, not forest-folk. It's still a bit of a mystery to me how you ever came in the first place but presumably you can escape and go back to your own land. I don't know why things have gone so wrong either. I've always trusted Trotter's word and he has always seemed to be right about the prophecies but... well, maybe he's misunderstood some things. What are we to do?'

'Listen, Stiggle,' Peter said. 'I know we're visitors, a bit like people from another planet and all that, but we're in this with you. Look, Aldred gave his life to save us; we would have died if it wasn't for his bravery and I feel a great debt to him. I think he had the right idea in attacking even if it didn't succeed fully. At least it's better than sitting around doing nothing. And there's Oswain. We can't just go away and forget he ever existed. No, we're willing to die, too, if necessary,' he concluded.

'Hear, hear, brother!'

The speaker was Andrew who had entered quietly and now stood looking rather pleased with himself, his hands behind his back.

'I agree, Pete. We've got to attack that witch together. And I've got something which will help us quite a lot,' he added.

They looked at him to see what it was.

'Well, what is it?' demanded Peter.

Slowly Andrew drew from behind his back a small, round, flatish object.

'Gilmere!' gasped Peter. 'Of course! How silly of me to forget. I'd assumed that wizard had got it.'

Andrew grinned from ear to ear.

'Well, I wondered about that but I thought I'd take a look just in case. It wasn't on the path, of course, and I was just going to give up when I saw it lying under a bush. I don't think I'd have found it if I'd not been really looking.'

'Great work, Andrew. At least we've got something on our side now. Things are looking up a bit. Come on, Stiggle. I think we should attack the castle and at least do as much damage as we can. Who knows, it might turn out better than we expect and old Trotter may be right about those prophecies after all.'

'Less of the old if you don't mind! And of course I'm right about the prophecies. Elmesh does not lie—even if it is all a bit confusing.'

They jumped at the sound of Trotter's voice as he and Sarah entered the room quietly through the study door. Both carried swords in their hands and were dressed in some sort of battle uniform.

'Hey, what's all this?' asked Peter.

'Quite simple,' his sister replied. 'Trotter and I are ready to fight Hagbane. And we're quite willing to go alone if you lot want to stay at home.'

'What?'

'Yes, we've decided it's gone too far to just sit around any more. We've nothing to lose, so we're going to fight. And we're ever so glad about the mirror, Andrew.'

She smiled sweetly at her younger brother but he could see the glint of determination in her eyes.

'Oh, er, yes…great. Yes, we've just come to the same conclusion—we fight. Glad you want to come along,' Peter said awkwardly. He wondered why it was that old folk and girls always seemed to be able to make their minds up quickly in a crisis.

'Right then,' cried Stiggle, feeling greatly encouraged now that a decision had been reached. 'To arms everyone. Let's prepare the troops!'

.   .   *   .   .

And so it was that a large company of forest-folk gathered together swiftly at Stiggle's call. This time they were in deadly earnest, ready to fight to the death, if needs be. Encouraged by Trotter's example, many older animals joined in, carrying ancient weapons. Swords, clubs, slings and staves were proudly carried as they assembled under Stiggle's command.

'Right, fall into ranks of six,' he ordered.

Everyone obeyed with much shuffling and good humour, particularly when Fumble managed to bring four others tumbling over with him as he tripped over his own stave.

'I give up!' groaned Grumble, who was one of those who had fallen.

Stiggle addressed his troops.

'We all know why we're here. If we don't defeat Hagbane we will be utter slaves for the rest of our lives, which she may shorten, in any case. We either accept that or we fight and maybe die in the attempt. This will be a fierce battle, with no quarter given, so if anyone wants to drop out, let him do so now.'

Silence descended on the company as he waited.

Nobody moved.

'All right, then let's go!' he cried. 'Death to Hagbane and all her evil! Vengeance for Aldred!'

'Forward, *march!*'

And so the motley army set off for the castle and whatever fate had in store for them.

. . * . .

Stiggle held up his hand to halt the company as they arrived in sight of the grim stone-walled fortress.

'Surprise is our best weapon, so we'll charge straight in. Those of you with ropes and grappling irons use them. Those who can climb walls anyway get up there as quickly as possible. It's important that we get the main gates open as soon as we can for the rest. Some of you, under Foxy's command are to take the tunnel entrance through which Peter escaped. I don't think they will expect us, so there may not be many guards on duty. Nevertheless, be ready for anything. Fight hard, and Elmesh go with you.'

He drew his sword and an eager murmur ran through the company. Nerves and sinews tightened as the thrill of battle gripped every heart.

'*Charge!*' yelled Stiggle, and the army surged forwards as one. They flooded across the open ground before the castle, shouting and yelling as they ran and brandishing their weapons.

Most were about halfway across the intervening space when, all of a sudden, the ground trembled beneath them. It heaved violently like a great earthen wave and many lost their balance. Fear and dismay filled their minds as they tottered about, imagining that Hagbane had been expecting them after all. Most thought they would be swallowed up alive at any moment.

An almighty crash came from within the castle walls and a vast sheet of flame shot into the sky. Everyone stared awe-struck at the sight. Another crash assailed their ears and the walls began to split and crumble. Fire roared from within.

'What's happening?' cried Peter.

'The prophecies are coming to pass, I believe,' Trotter replied quietly as he lay beside him on the still shaky ground. 'I think the Merestone has been made whole at last.'

The walls continued to crash down before them and they saw dark Grogs fleeing for their lives.

'Get them!' Stiggle commanded as he regained some control over the situation. 'Attack now, while we have the chance.'

The animals rose to the order and streaked after the fleeing guards. At that moment, a terrifying screech rent the air from high in the sky, chilling the blood with its eeriness and fury. They stared upwards.

'It's Arca!' cried Sarah. 'Hurrah! He's come to help us.'

The mighty eagle swooped low, fearsome talons outstretched, his shadow racing across the ground. Terrified Grogs fell before his wrath, never to rise again. No mercy did he show to these cruel creatures who had hurt so many of the forest-folk.

Sarah grabbed the mirror from Peter.

'You use your sword. I'll take this.'

Before he could argue she was gone into the thick of the battle. Weapons clashed, shouts and groans filled the air, smoke and dust choked the lungs, but on rushed Sarah towards the castle, intent on facing the witch herself. She reached the walls and began to clamber over the rubble. Suddenly, a Grog blocked her way. He raised a great sword and prepared to strike. Sarah flicked open Gilmere. The light blazed forth and her foe shrivelled to a cinder before her gaze. Moments later she was standing in the courtyard. Buildings blazed all around her and massive beams fell in showers of sparks. Smoke swirled everywhere and Sarah looked about her vainly to get some bearings.

The next moment, a huge, dark shadow fell across her. She turned. There before her reared a gigantic Grim, like some prehistoric monster, with its fierce taloned wings outstretched, black as night. Its eyes glared red with hate. The long jaws snapped greedily. Sarah fumbled with the mirror, almost dropping it. The light streamed forth—and missed! Her mouth dropped open with dismay as the loathsome creature advanced on her. She screamed and the mirror fell from her nerveless fingers, its light still blazing.

Then, just as the vile creature was about to strike, the ground shook and where the light of the mirror shone a vast chasm opened. With a scream of rage the creature fell into its depths. Sarah lay panting and gasping, her heart beating fit to burst. She shook with fear and her legs refused to hold her weight. Vainly, she looked around for the mirror but realized, to her dismay, that it too had fallen into the abyss. She knew now that she had no weapon with which to face Hagbane. She arose slowly, a firm resolve filling her.

'Then I will have to face her alone, in the name of Elmesh,' she muttered to herself.

A door hung crazily from its broken hinges and she

stumbled resolutely towards it, heedless of the chaos about her.

.　　.　　*　　.　　.

'Stiggle, Stiggle, we're winning!' Peter grinned triumphantly at the weasel as they struggled towards the castle.

'Yes,' he shouted in reply. 'I reckon we've got them on the run. Oswain must be behind this somehow, you know. I wonder what he's done?'

'We'll find out soon enough now,' his comrade replied. 'Looks like the prophecies were right after all.'

It was not long before all the Grogs had been dealt with and the noise of battle began to quieten down. Hagbane's castle was utterly ruined. Peter, Andrew and Stiggle climbed over the broken walls and entered the wrecked courtyard.

'Phew, what a mess!' Andrew exclaimed.

'I wonder where Oswain is? And Sarah too,' said Peter. 'They must be around here somewhere. Give them a yell, will you?'

'Sarah? Oswain? Where are you?'

There was no reply to their call. They stood silently.

'Hush! What's that?' said Stiggle.

They listened and heard the sound of sobbing.

'That's Sarah. Quickly, it's coming from over there.'

Joined by Trotter, they ran across the yard and entered a room which had obviously been Hagbane's lair. There they found Sarah, begrimed with soot, sitting on the floor sobbing. Before her yawned a wide chasm from which came a dull red glow and a subterranean roar, muted by the distance. Sarah turned at the sound of their coming, her tears making white streaks down her blackened cheeks. She looked at them in anguish.

'He's dead,' she wailed. 'I know it. And Hagbane too. They've fallen down there—into that awful pit.'

She pointed into the deep gaping hole.

'Oh, why did it have to happen like this? He's destroyed her but he's died too. We've won but we've lost really.'

And with that she burst into tears again. The rest advanced slowly towards her, peering gingerly at the great rift in the floor. Peter put his arm around his sister. Suddenly he felt very weary. Together they gazed glumly into the chasm but it was too deep to see anything except the red glow.

'Come on, Sis, it's no use staying here,' said Peter quietly and he helped her to her feet.

Chapter Eighteen

TO THE ENCHANTED GLADE

Before anyone could do much else, the room was shaken by a deep rumble. Dust fell all about them and half-burned timbers groaned under their load. Fresh fears flooded into the weary souls gathered there and they expected to be buried alive at any moment. Then, as they fell about in confusion, trying to protect themselves from the falling masonry, they saw the yawning chasm begin to close up. A final crash, which brought even more debris down, and only a jagged line indicated that anything had ever been there. The rumbling and the shaking ceased as suddenly as it had commenced. Everyone stood coughing in the dust, staring at the crack across the floor.

'It's closed up,' said Andrew rather obviously.

'Yes, that's that then, I suppose,' Peter replied. 'Nothing more we can do. Though goodness knows what that pit was. It seemed to go on for ever like some kind of hell. It was horrible.'

'I confess that I do not understand it,' said Trotter. 'Except that Oswain seemed to know what he was doing when he handed himself over to Hagbane. There may be more to it yet, but I am at a loss to know what.'

At that moment, one of the roof beams began to

groan and bend.

'Come on,' cried Stiggle. 'We'd better get out of here. This room isn't safe. Anyway, we must tell the others.'

With that they made for the door and escaped only just in time before most of the ceiling collapsed. As they came into sight a vast cheer arose from the animals assembled in the courtyard.

'Hurrah for Stiggle! Hurrah for Peter!'

'Hurrah for Andrew! For Sarah!'

'Hurrah for Trotter!'

They stood together and smiled wanly at the company before them. Trotter raised a paw to indicate quiet so he could speak. He stepped forward and cleared his throat.

'My dear forest-folk,' he began. 'You have every good reason to be happy, for a mighty victory has been obtained here today. All the Grogs and Grims have been destroyed thanks to your bravery and the assistance of Arca.'

He was interrupted by much cheering and clapping, particularly for the eagle, who was perched on a remaining part of the wall. Trotter waved for silence again.

'The best news of all which I have for you is that Hagbane herself is dead.'

For a brief instant there was silence, then, as the truth sank in, the whole crowd erupted into cheering, foot-stamping, shouting and whistling. Animals danced with glee and it looked as if celebrations were about to start there and then, even though there was no food and nobody was exactly dressed for the occasion. Trotter waited patiently until things quietened down a little. Even those who knew what had become of Oswain could not resist smiling as they saw the joy and relief on the animals' faces. Eventually, Trotter continued.

'We are free at last to live our lives in peace without fear of arrest or death. I cannot put into words just how much that means to us all.' His voice trembled with emotion. 'But, it has not been without its cost. I see some of you have been wounded in the fighting, though no one has died, but I refer especially to our dear brave Aldred who longed for this day, and . . . and to Oswain.'

He faltered and a murmur ran through the crowd.

'Yes, I am afraid Oswain is dead too,' he said at last. 'It appears that he died while destroying Hagbane, but I cannot say what happened exactly. The truth is, we have received some remarkable help from Elmesh. Were it not for the earthquake things might have been very different. Part of that earthquake split the ground in Hagbane's lair and it appears that both fell to their doom. We owe a great debt to Oswain's memory for he willingly paid the ultimate price for our freedom.'

A solemn silence had fallen over the audience as the full meaning began to sink in.

'Well,' said Trotter, brightening up. 'What's done is done and I am sure it is what Elmesh wished, so, go to your homes. Tell your loved ones and your children that they are free to enjoy the Forest once more. May Elmesh bless you all . . . and thank you for all you have done today.'

The crowd slowly dispersed, everybody talking amongst themselves about the events of the day, and soon only the little band of five was left.

'We'll pull this castle right down,' said Stiggle. 'Then we'll erect a monument to Aldred and Oswain's memory. It'll become a favourite spot, I expect.'

'That's a good idea,' Andrew said. 'You could use the stones of the castle to build it.'

'I think I would just like to get away from this place at the moment,' said Sarah. 'Can we go?'

'I think Sarah's right,' said Peter. 'Come on everyone. We look as though we could do with a wash and brush-up, let alone something to eat. I'm starving.'

They looked at their bedraggled clothes and grimy faces and then burst out laughing.

'We do look a sight. I wonder what Mrs Trotter will say?' chuckled Trotter. 'Yes, let us get back and leave all our problems for the moment. Things have not been so good in years.'

Andrew spoke to Sarah as they walked slowly back.

'Maybe that's all there is to it, Sarah. We've done our part and perhaps we can go home to Mum and Dad now. I know you're upset over Oswain, but maybe he's done his part, too.'

'I don't know,' his sister replied. 'It feels so incomplete, so...well...so, not right, if you know what I mean?'

'Yes, I do. But you mustn't let it get you down. Come on, race you back to the cottage.'

'Thanks. I'll try not to be too sad. But I think I'll walk back, if you don't mind.'

.   .   *   .   .

By the time everybody had eaten and cleaned themselves up, it was quite late. Nobody needed any encouragement to go to bed and it was not long before they were all sound asleep. All, that is, save for old

Trotter. The badger was perplexed and sat up long into the night staring straight ahead, lost in thought. Much later, he arose and went to his library where he began to pore over some dusty parchments.

'It doesn't make sense,' he muttered to himself over and over again. 'I wonder? I just wonder?'

It was not until the early hours of the morning that he eventually stopped and fell asleep in his armchair with the papers sprawled across his lap.

.   .   *   .   .

Around five o'clock that same morning Trotter awoke with a jerk. Outside he could hear the birds singing and the sun was already up. Swiftly and silently he got up and left the house. The air outside was fresh and sweet and he could not help but notice that the vegetation was looking fresher than he could ever remember seeing it, even back in the old days before the troubles began. Bright green leaves shed a delicate filigree of shadows over the path as he walked. He breathed deeply of the wholesome air, then made his way resolutely towards the enchanted glade.

Sarah had slept heavily and dreamlessly but she also woke up quite suddenly not long after Trotter had left. She got up quietly, noting that everyone was asleep but that somebody had gone out of the house, leaving the door ajar. She felt sure it was Trotter and that he was on his way to the glade. With scarcely a moment's hesitation she determined to follow him.

Trotter sat down upon a moss-covered rock in the enchanted glade. The air seemed electric all around him and he felt a tingle of joy running through his old frame. It was as though the years were falling off and he was young again. He heard a rustle behind him and leapt to his feet.

'Oh, it's you, Sarah,' he said with a slight tinge of disappointment in his voice. 'I had expected someone else. But then, I am not surprised that we should be here together again.'

'Hallo,' she whispered. 'I just had to come. I've got this feeling that, well...that something very wonderful is going to happen today. I just know it but I can't explain it.'

'There is no need to try, child, I feel exactly the same. That is why I am here. There are things I did not understand when I read the old writings last night, but when I awoke this morning I knew that I must come here and wait. Hush! What is that?'

He placed his paw on Sarah's shoulder.

'It came from over there, from Elmere itself.'

They gazed in the direction of the pool but nothing seemed to have changed. Still the pearl-like droplets dripped from the overhanging ledge with their musical plip-plop. Then Sarah cried out: 'The water! Look, it's moving!'

They rushed towards the pool and, sure enough, its surface was in tremendous turmoil. It began to boil and splash until slowly a shape began to rise from its depths. The two watchers stood transfixed. The shape became the figure of a man who rose splashing from the water. An aura of light seemed to surround him and he was magnificently clothed in purple and gold, glistening with wetness. He rubbed his eyes with his hands then looked around him. The full morning sun captured his strong tanned features and penetrating eyes.

'It's Oswain!' cried Sarah. 'It's Oswain! He's come back!'

Sarah raced towards him and threw her arms about his neck.

'Oh, Oswain, it's you! It's really you!' she exclaimed.

For a moment he looked surprised and then laughed.

'Sarah! I thought you were dead! Yes, it is me. All has come to pass as promised.'

'So I was right,' breathed the badger. 'Welcome back, Oswain, Son of the High King and rightful Ruler of the Forest.'

He knelt before the man but Oswain swiftly reached out a hand and lifted him to his feet.

'Trotter, old friend, King I am, as it is written, but I will not have one such as you bowing before me. I count you an equal, not a servant. But how delightful this is, to be greeted by you two on my return. And you alive, Sarah. I can't tell you how happy all this makes me. And what a beautiful morning too!'

He laughed again and soon all three of them were delirious with joy, dancing round and round with their arms thrown about each other.

'B..b..but how? W...what happened?' puffed Sarah as they eventually quietened down. 'How did you kill Hagbane? How did you get here? And... and...'

'Enough, Sarah. I shall tell you all just as soon as everyone is gathered together. It won't do to spoil it now, will it? How are Peter and Andrew? Is everyone all right?'

'Yes, everyone is well except for... but I will tell you later,' declared Trotter. 'They will all be overjoyed to meet you again. Why, this is truly amazing. I can hardly wait to hear your explanations myself.'

'Well, that will not be long now, and then I will hear the story of what has happened to you. But there is more to happen yet. Come over here, I want you to see this.'

He led them across to the pool and plunged his hand into the water. Slowly, he drew forth a glittering jewel and held it up in the light for them to see. The stone glowed with brilliant fire and its power radiated right through their very beings. Were it not for Oswain's presence, Sarah felt she would have been crushed by its influence.

'The Merestone,' sighed Trotter. 'You have the Merestone. After all these years.'

Tears came to the old badger's eyes as he gazed upon the jewel. Memories of the past flooded back and he knew that his life's dream was fulfilled.

'Yes,' replied Oswain. 'And now I restore the Merestone to its rightful place, that it may never be removed again while a king reigns in the Great Forest.'

So saying, he placed the jewel upon the rock to the side of the pool. There was a hissing sound and the stone fixed firm. He tapped it.

'There. It is done. From this day the Forest will be blessed by its presence and the latter days will be as glorious as the former.'

The three gazed reverently upon Elmesh's stone, entranced by its beauty and power.

'Can we go now?' asked Sarah. 'I'm dying to tell the others.'

'I think we may,' Oswain replied. 'Listen though. I hear the sound of footsteps.'

Chapter Nineteen

EXPLANATIONS

Peter's eyes opened; he blinked and, twisting in his bed, looked around him at the familiar warm room. Sunlight was streaming through the leaded windows, lighting the old oak furniture with a mellow glow. He could smell the freshness of one of those days when you just have to get out of bed.

'Hey, come on everybody,' he shouted, 'time to get up.'

He gave his brother a shove.

'Wassermarra?' Andrew groaned sleepily. 'What time is it?'

'Getting up time! It's a smashing day. Come on!'

Andrew was not yet convinced. He snuggled into the blankets while Peter went into the other rooms to wake the rest.

'Hey, where's Sarah and Trotter?' he called. 'They're not here.'

'Oh, they've gone out, my dear,' called Mrs Trotter from her room. 'To the enchanted glade, I expect, if I know them.'

'The enchanted glade? We'd better go after them then. Don't want to miss anything. Come on, Andrew. Get a move on. We'd better hurry.'

By now Andrew was wide awake too.

'All right, but how do we get there? I don't think I know the way.'

'Nor do I, but I reckon we'll be okay today. I just feel it.'

'I'll have breakfast waiting for you all,' Mrs Trotter called as they made for the door. 'Mind you're not too long now.'

Outside, dew sparkled in the early sunshine, birds chirped in the trees which were fresh with newly-opened leaves. The sky was blue, the air was clean and it felt good to be alive.

'I can't believe this,' cried Andrew. 'Yesterday, we were in the thick of battle and mourning Oswain but today I don't feel tired or aching or . . . or even sad.'

'Yes, I feel the same,' his brother replied. 'Something good has happened in the night. Perhaps it's just that Hagbane is dead and the curse is lifted. Anyway, Trotter's bound to know. Come on. The path starts here. Race you to the glade!'

So off they ran and, sure enough, they did find all the right paths and it was not long before they arrived, puffing and panting, at the great sentinel stones which marked the entrance to the glade. Peter made it only just ahead of his brother.

'Come on, slowcoach! Let's find the others.'

They stepped into the glade just as Sarah, Trotter and Oswain turned to their sound.

'Hi Sarah! Hi Tro . . .'

The boys stood speechless with their mouths hanging open in amazement. For a moment they just stared and stared. Andrew was the first to regain his voice.

'Oswain! Oswain? It is you isn't it? B . . . but, we

thought you were dead.'

'And so I was,' he replied. 'But I have returned from the darkness. Hallo Andrew—and Peter. It is a great joy to see you here.'

Slowly, the two boys came forward. Actually, they both felt just a little bit awkward, though afterwards neither could explain why.

'It *is* you, Oswain,' Peter whispered. 'I'm so glad. We really did think you were dead and ... and that was all. It was so horrible.'

There were tears in his eyes as he spoke and Oswain put his arms around the shoulders of the two boys.

'I have a lot to explain to you and I'll do that just as soon as—well, just as soon as we have had breakfast. To tell you the truth, I'm very hungry '

He laughed and the awkwardness was broken. They all began to laugh together and it was a jolly company which romped its way back to the cottage.

Upon their arrival, they found Stiggle awaiting them. He bowed low before Oswain as soon as he realized who he was. The poor weasel could not cope with Sarah's garbled explanations and stood, as the boys had done, quite speechless.

'Stiggle, I am glad to see you, but where is your brave captain, Aldred?'

At this, a solemnity fell upon them all. Trotter spoke:

'Sire, Aldred, Aldred our brave captain, has died. He gave his life to save those of the children when they were almost burnt alive.'

Oswain was silent for a long time upon hearing this news.

'He was a courageous leader. He shall not be forgotten. You must relate to me the whole story. His

166

name shall be honoured throughout my kingdom.'

They were interrupted at this point by Mrs Trotter who came bustling out of the door. Trotter hurried across to his wife and briefly explained what had happened. She advanced slowly and curtsied low before Oswain.

'I've already laid an extra place for you, sir. I rather thought you might come back.'

Oswain smiled.

'Arise, great and noble lady of the Forest! Trotter, you have a fine wife. She does you proud. Come now, let us eat and do justice to her labours!'

After an enormous breakfast during which little was said to interrupt the serious business of eating, everyone strolled outside and sat in a circle on the warm grass. Eagerly, they looked to Oswain as he began his promised explanation of what had taken place.

'The early history of the Great Forest I will not repeat to you,' he began. 'For you know all that is necessary including the time when Hagbane seized the Merestone and began her evil reign. But I must take you back to a time before that, to the time of my youth in my own land of the West.

'My Father is King of that land, which has been a great kingdom for many an age. He is both wise and good and has seen to it that I should have a fine upbringing which would fit me to succeed him one day. It is the custom in my country for the wise to speak words of good counsel to the young and, on occasion, to predict their path. Such was my case and it was known that not only should I inherit my father's kingdom but that a time would come when I should become legal ruler of the Great Forest beyond the mountains. It was said that this was by the will of

Elmesh and that he would make known to me the day when this should be. It was also revealed to me that it would involve sacrifice and suffering to achieve this. I may say that I did not relish the idea at all.

'And then the day came, or I should say the night, for it was given to me in a fearsome dream. Elmesh spoke in a vision and I knew my time had come. So I set out for my unknown destiny.'

'That would be when I also heard from Elmesh,' interrupted Trotter.

'Yes, and Arca too. When it is time Elmesh speaks to many so that there need be no doubt.'

'And then we came down the tree!' exclaimed Andrew. 'But we didn't know why until Trotter explained things to us. And mighty strange that seemed!'

'I'm sure it did,' Oswain laughed. 'It is strange enough when you know something of Elmesh's ways but even more so for you who had not heard his name before.'

'You saw something in the Star Pool,' said Sarah. 'I think I know what, but please tell us.'

'Ah, yes, Sarah. You have a special gift indeed. Much as the wise of my own land. Beware lest you grow too old to recognize it any more, child, for it is given to few.

'Now, when I reached the Forest—which I only managed after strong opposition from dark forces—I discovered that Hagbane was the foe but I was unprepared for what should follow. I gazed into Elmere that time when you found me, Sarah, and I saw the truth. I had known Hagbane before. She is the one I was to have married.'

All but Sarah gasped at this.

'Phew! No wonder you didn't want to talk about it,' Peter murmured.

'But she was surely not always like that?' queried Trotter.

'No indeed,' Oswain replied. 'She was once the fairest maid in the Wester lands. And my heart was lost to her, so greatly did I love her. She was to become my wife and future queen of my kingdom.'

'Then what happened?' Stiggle asked.

'I spoke to you before of the great evil which seemed to fall upon the land. It was a time of disturbance and fear. Strangers came in great numbers through our country and it was one of these who poisoned my beloved's heart. Some evil seed of pride and greed possessed her and she became a changed creature. In those days, I should say, she was named Dorinda. My Dorinda began to behave strangely. She became hard and arrogant. She wanted things—gold, silver, servants. She became unbearable and my heart broke as I saw the change.

'At length, my parents decided that she was unfit to be my bride and our engagement was broken. Dorinda was furious and swore vengeance but then she went away for a long while.'

'That must have been when she came to the Great Forest and stole the Merestone,' said Trotter.

'Indeed. And she returned with it to my land, more evil than ever. She knew, of course, of the prophecies concerning my rule over the Forest and I think this was her vengeance, that she should possess this fair realm for herself.

'My mother, who is a wise woman, surmised this and confronted Dorinda. This was also shown me in the Pool. She attempted to wrest the Merestone from her but failed, for Dorinda had gained some power of which my mother did not know. She was defeated, but in the conflict the Merestone was dropped and a splinter broke off. This my mother had mounted in a ring and placed it upon my finger, sure that the day would come when the Merestone would be reunited. Little were we to know how that should be,' he said sadly.

'And Hagbane—I mean, Dorinda—left your land?' Peter asked.

'Yes, and came to dominate this Forest. Here the evil seed fully possessed her heart and she became the Hagbane whom you knew so well.'

'It must have been terrible for you to know that she was your enemy,' Sarah said.

'And you knew you had to meet her, which is why you let yourself be captured,' said Trotter.

'That is correct, though I never imagined that it would be in such horrifying circumstances for you children. Now you must tell me what happened after that, for I was borne away in great anguish for your safety.'

Between them they told Oswain of the subsequent events, particularly of Aldred's sacrifice, upon the hearing of which Oswain wept. They spoke of the battle and of their discovery of Oswain's death. All were eager to know of the events within the castle. Oswain told them of Hagbane's terrible sceptre and of her attempt to use it to conquer him.

'I beseeched her to give up this madness but she had gone too far. I saw that nothing would change her and knew that I could love Dorinda no more, for she had become Hagbane for ever.

'It was then that she made her mistake. She brought

forth the Merestone to add power to her sceptre. But the stone had originated with Elmesh and it was his time. The stone reunited and Elmesh wreaked his vengeance and brought to pass his will. The room flared and the earthquake occurred. Just as you thought, Sarah, we fell together into the abyss, locked in mortal combat.'

'Then why didn't you die? I mean, why are you here?' Andrew asked. 'I don't understand that at all.'

'I cannot fully explain all that took place in the terrible depths of that pit, but we did not die, as you understand death. Great forces were unleashed, light against darkness, good against evil, life against death. We ceased to be bodies as you know them but the battle continued until with my spirit I grasped the Merestone as mine by right and Hagbane...Hagbane was destroyed.

'I was much wearied by the struggle and wandered as a spirit through the darkness beneath the earth, only the light and hope of the Merestone guiding me. None dared touch me in that shadowy realm. Slowly my strength returned and I was renewed until I heard the very voice of Elmesh call me forth to life. I came to the Star Pool whence the light of El-la met that of the Merestone once more and in that glory I received my body again and came forth from the waters as you beheld.' He smiled towards Trotter and Sarah.

'Yes,' Trotter spoke. 'I *knew* that something must happen. The prophecies had been right all along and I could not believe they would fail now. I studied them again until sleep overtook me. When I awoke I knew the answer lay in the glade and so I came to await whatever should come to pass.'

'I think it's utterly amazing,' Peter declared. 'Why,

I've never heard of anything so...'

'Quick!'

Stiggle cried out and leapt to his feet. Before anyone else could move he shot into the bushes and began crashing around. Moments later he emerged carrying a torn piece of green cloth in his paw.

'Pah! Too late. They got away.'

'What's all that about?' said Andrew.

'Hey, I recognize that cloth,' cried Peter.

'It's the wizard's!' Sarah gasped.

'Yes,' Stiggle replied. 'I heard a rustle in the bushes. We weasels have excellent hearing, you know. They must have been listening. Pity I wasn't a bit quicker.'

'Never mind,' Oswain said. 'They heard little to their good. I guess two wizards are, at this very moment, fleeing for their lives. They know now this is no place to be. Poor shadows!'

.   .   *   .   .

Deep in the undergrowth, two figures scuttled along as fast as their legs could carry them. The taller one slapped the other around his bald head.

'You stupid idiot. Why can't you keep quiet? They'll be after us now.'

'It's not my fault, you gawky old fool. I don't know why we had to go spying again, anyway. It would have made more sense to have tried getting on their side.'

'Bah! You know nothing,' Terras replied. 'You don't think that they would have the likes of us, do you? Come on, let's get out of here before it's too late.'

And so, still grumbling at each other, the two wizards

fled the Forest to seek their fortune elsewhere. But, high in the sky, a pair of fierce eagle eyes watched their going and their direction.

Chapter Twenty

CELEBRATIONS

Oswain's return was greeted at first by sheer unbelief by many of the forest-folk but, as they came to see him, their incredulity changed to great joy. The discovery, too, that the Merestone was back in its rightful place was a source of tremendous security, and day after day animals made pilgrimage to the enchanted glade (which was more wonderful than ever) to gaze in reverence upon that source of Elmesh's blessing upon their lives.

And so the tale is nearly told. The Great Forest prospered and flourished under the long and happy reign of Oswain. Animals walked without fear; the young pranced about with not a care in the world; food grew in abundance and everyone said it was the happiest place there ever was. All traces of Hagbane's rule were swiftly and thoroughly erased—the stones of her castle became all sorts of useful things, such as a new jetty for the river, paths, house walls and mill-stones. Elmere became again the place for wisdom, for healing, for young lovers to promise to be true to each other.

All this came about as a matter of time but there was one early event which stayed in everyone's heart and formed a topic of conversation for many years to come. It was the great celebration.

For days following Oswain's return there was much planning and activity on the part of the forest-folk. Even the children were drafted in to help Mrs Trotter with the baking. Rumour had it that this was to be the biggest feast ever!

At last the day came and everybody gathered together in the old clearing. And how different it was from their last meeting. The sun shone upon the fresh green grass; trees proudly displayed their blossomed finery; flowers, gorgeous in colour and exotic in fragrance, filled every available spot. The air buzzed with excitement as the multitude came together. Young eyes looked longingly at the heavily-laden food tables and hoped that the formalities would not take too long.

Then a long, cool, clear trumpet sounded. Everyone turned their attention to the dais which had been erected for the occasion. Trotter stepped forward and spoke.

'My dear forest-folk,' he began, 'I want to welcome you all to this great occasion, this time of celebration, of thanksgiving and of feasting.'

He paused as everyone cheered wildly. He held up his paw for silence.

'For long years now, in fact, longer than I can remember, I have had the privilege of being your leader. Those years were hard and sad and only by the help of Elmesh was I able to keep going. My hope lay in the promise of deliverance which was given in the elder days. Good folk, that deliverance has come and we are once more free. Elmesh be praised!'

More cheering rent the air.

'Now, my time as your leader is completed. My task is done. It is my joy to appoint one to succeed me as Ruler whom we can utterly trust to be wise and just. To you who dwell in the realm of the Great Forest, I present, Oswain, the Son of the High King of the West, whom I declare your King by the will of Elmesh!'

The tall, gracious figure of Oswain rose and stepped forward, resplendent in his royal robes. He stood, noble features caught in the sunlight, and smiled upon the crowd. All bowed before his majesty. He spoke in a deep, clear voice.

'Rise, forest-folk, for I will not have you in fear of me. My reign must be one of love and friendship, of justice and truth, not pomp and ceremony nor threat and fear. We shall begin as we intend to continue.'

'Hear, hear,' said an old rabbit.

'Soon we shall eat and drink and celebrate together.'

More cheers, especially from the younger element in the crowd.

'But first,' he continued. 'We must express our gratitude and thanks to those who have brought us to this happy day. The foremost is old Trotter himself. For long years he has been a faithful adviser and friend to you all. It was he who saw the time of Elmesh's visitation. He is the one who so fearlessly campaigned against Hagbane's evil devices. None can put into words how much he has done for the Forest. He has stood down from leadership but I cannot fully let that be. Friends, I wish to appoint Trotter as my chief and personal advisor for the rest of his days—and may they and those of his wife be long and happy. They shall be Lord and Lady Trotter.'

The whole crowd rose as one and applauded this announcement, while Trotter looked a bit abashed, but nonetheless obviously pleased.

'Next,' Oswain continued. 'There are three very brave mice. Fumble, Mumble and Grumble, come forward!'

There was a rustling at the front of the crowd.

'Ouch! Silly clot! Can't you do it right even today? Get off my foot!'

'Sorry,' Fumble replied, still standing on it.

'Cumonutoo, stomonin, erwaing.'

'Oh, shush!'

The three mice made their way up the steps and bowed low before the King, only Fumble bowed so low he fell over in a somersault and landed on his back, legs waving in the air. Everyone burst out laughing, much to Grumble's indignation.

'Fumble, Mumble and Grumble,' Oswain continued, once order had been restored. 'In token of your bravery I make you knights of honour to accompany me wherever I go.'

The mice swelled with pride, whilst Trotter looked a little alarmed.

'Don't worry,' whispered Oswain to him. 'I shall send them to the enchanted glade until their, um, difficulties have been sorted out. But they are of fine heart, old friend, do not fear.'

He turned to address the crowd once more.

'We have had a mighty ally, without whom we could not have achieved this victory and we must thank him.'

So saying, Oswain raised his eyes heavenwards and whistled long and shrill. From his lofty domain Arca, the mighty white eagle, plummeted to earth. With wings outspread he glided gracefully to land before the King. Although the animals knew him to be a friend they, nonetheless, drew back before his might.

'Arca, we thank you for all you have done. I give you no reward for I know you would take none. And I ask no allegiance of you for I know you serve Elmesh alone. But I bid you always welcome amongst us and would have you know of the honour with which you are held in all our hearts.'

'It is well,' the bird croaked in reply. 'Elmesh's will has been done. May his sun warm your days and the light of El-la guard your nights. Farewell, Oswain. May your reign be long and peaceful.'

With a shrill screech, the eagle rose from the ground and climbed upwards towards the sun until not even the keenest eyes could follow him.

'And now, good folk, I give you the children, Peter, Sarah and Andrew.'

The three children came forward slowly and mounted the steps. Everyone rose again and cheered so enthusiastically that they felt quite embarrassed.

'These came from far beyond the Forest, even from another realm. They are here at Elmesh's bidding and found themselves unwittingly caught up in our battles. Many fearsome dangers they have faced in the struggle but they have remained brave and loyal. They are an example to us all and we express our gratitude to them for all they have done. But soon they must return to their own land and time. I cannot bid them stay, though I gladly would, but I would have them remember us and know of our thanks.'

Oswain motioned to Trotter and the latter brought forth a velvet covered tray upon which there lay three transluscent pearls of crystal. Each had a chain of gold so fine as to be almost invisible. Oswain passed one around the neck of each child in turn.

'These are solidified droplets from Elmere,' he explained. 'At least, as near as can be called solidified, for you will find that they possess a life and a power more than sight or touch can tell. Take them as our token of thanks.'

Sarah and Andrew looked at Peter and nodded to him to say something. He blushed, coughed, cleared his throat and began:

'Er, um, well I don't know what to say really, but, er, thanks for everthing. It's been a wonderful adventure but scary too and, um, well, I'm, I mean, we're glad it turned out all right in the end. And we think you really are wonderful and . . . and we're really glad this happened to us.'

He finished, still a bit flushed. The crowd applauded loudly as the three resumed their seats.

'Well done, Pete,' Andrew whispered. 'I wouldn't have known what to say.'

'Look at these jewels,' Sarah said. 'Why, you can hardly see them they're so clear. I think they're beautiful and mine makes me feel all kind of special.'

Oswain was speaking again.

'There is one more person to mention,' he declared. 'And I have left him to last because of his importance. I refer, of course, to our brave and noble captain, Aldred. Alas, he is no longer with us, as you all know. He gave his life to save the children as selflessly as he had lived and fought. We mourn his loss but his name shall always be honoured and remembered in our midst.'

He pointed to a large object covered with a white sheet. All had been wondering what it was but great secrecy had surrounded the project, although the sound of hammering and chiselling had been heard.

Oswain motioned with his hand and four young stoats tugged at the sheet. It fell off amid wondering gasps. Revealed in shining stone was a larger than life statue of Aldred mounted upon a pedestal of rough-hewn rock. It really was a most magnificent sculpture and a worthy monument of the brave leader.

'From now on,' cried Oswain. 'This clearing shall be known as Aldred's Park and thus shall his name be perpetuated for ever.'

A heartfelt round of applause greeted this proclamation.

'And now,' he smiled at the folk gathered before him, 'the time has come to end the formalities and to commence the feasting. Let us then make merry!'

Possibly the loudest cheer went up at that moment, especially from the younger ones, and the crowd descended upon the food-laden tables.

.   .   *   .   .

Peter, Sarah and Andrew were sitting together in the shade of a tree about two hours later, having eaten their fill of goodies and spoken to innumerable animals who wanted to thank them personally.

'Phew, I feel blown,' declared Andrew.

'Me too,' his brother agreed. 'This has certainly been some party. I wonder what time it will end?'

'I don't know,' said Sarah. 'Probably quite late, I should think. But I feel it's finished for us now, anyway. We've done what we were sent to do and I kind of feel, well, an outsider again. Do you know what I mean?'

'Yes, I agree,' nodded Peter. 'I think we shall go soon. It feels a bit sad but we really must get back to our own home.'

'I suppose we can do that,' said Andrew, a little anxiously. 'I mean...'

'Oh, of course we can,' his sister interrupted. 'If Elmesh got us here he can get us back. I'm not worried anyway.'

'You know, it seems bad but I've hardly thought about Mum and Dad, but I guess they'll be terribly worried about us. Do you think they'll be angry when they see us?' Peter said.

'No, just relieved,' Sarah replied.

'I bet they've had the police out, and tracker dogs and helicopters and the army and everything,' Andrew enthused.

'Oh, I do hope not,' said Sarah.

'Well, we'll find out soon enough now,' said Peter. 'Here comes Oswain and Trotter and I have the feeling it's going to be time to say goodbye.'

They rose to their feet as the King and the badger drew near.

Chapter Twenty-one

RETURN TO THE OLD OAK

The afternoon shadows were lengthening in the slowly
sinking sun and the air was warm and sweet with the
scent of honeysuckle as the little company wended its
way through the Forest paths. It had been decided in
the end that only a few should see the children off and
so, after touching farewells to the animals and
especially to Fumble, Mumble and Grumble, only
Oswain, Trotter, Mrs Trotter and Stiggle accompanied
them on this last walk through the Forest.

Together, they had stood for a while before the
monument to Aldred. Tears had flowed freely as they
remembered how he had saved them from a horrible
death, only to lose his own life. Then they had paid a
last visit to the enchanted glade. Here, joy had filled
their hearts once more as the magic of Elmere lifted
their heaviness. The Merestone radiated a soft warmth
which filled the air with life and goodness, while its
light now gave the dripping water a greater glory than
before.

'My, this is a wonderful place,' Peter had declared,
overcome by joy. 'I could stay here for ever!'

'Yes, hasn't it all been worth it,' his brother had
agreed.

And to this they had all heartily concurred before setting out to seek a single oak tree.

. . * . .

'Just around here, I think,' said Trotter, breaking the silence of the last few hundred metres.

They rounded a clump of bushes and there before them stood a tall English Oak, stately and leaf-laden, the late afternoon sun shimmering through its branches in dappled shades of green. There too was Sarah's red ribbon, the one she had left so that they could find the right tree again, and she ran across to retrieve it. Slowly, they walked to the base of the mighty trunk, rounded it and came upon the hole which led upwards.

'Well, here are are,' said Peter with a sigh.

They stood in an awkward silence for a few moments, until Oswain spoke.

'Peter, Sarah, Andrew, we have become great friends in the brief time we have known one another and it is not at all easy to say farewell. However, it is the will of Elmesh that you should leave and so return you must.'

'Oh, I wish I could stay for ever!' Sarah exclaimed. 'I love it so much now it's all changed. And you have become such dear friends. If only we could come back when we pleased, but I know it's not like that.'

She bent and kissed first Mrs Trotter and then Trotter himself.

'I shall never forget you. And thank you for looking after us.'

'I don't know that I did much of that, my dear,' said Mrs Trotter. 'Seems to me that there were others who protected you when you needed it.'

'Yes, but you made it all so warm and homely.'

Stiggle she hugged and Oswain stooped and put his arm around her.

'Sarah, you and I have a special kind of kinship, for you possess the same gift as my mother. Guard it well and use it wisely to help others. Do not let the passing years snatch it from you.'

She looked into his deep, serious eyes and nodded. Tears filled her own as he kissed her goodbye.

The two boys shook hands with the badgers and the weasel as cheerily as they could and they all wished each other well. Oswain put his arms around their shoulders.

'Boys, you have played a valiant part in this adventure, with courage far beyond your years, and you have learned many lessons about the ways of good and evil. Do not forget these as you grow up. It will not be the last time you are called upon by Elmesh, of that I am sure. Farewell, my good friends.'

Peter and Andrew said their farewells, feeling suddenly very grown up.

'Right then,' said Peter. 'Everyone ready? Let's go.'

And so the three entered the warm darkness of the oak tree, waving goodbye to the four who watched their departure.

'Here are the steps,' said Andrew and began to climb.

Upwards they toiled into the darkness until a faint glow of light showed ahead of them.

'Nearly there,' puffed Peter.

Each felt it again at the same point: a strange tingling sensation all over which told them they had passed through some invisible barrier. Seven steps later and they were in the short tunnel. The next instant they were looking down upon their uncle's orchard in the late afternoon sun.

'I wonder what day it is?' Sarah thought.

'Mum and Dad are going to be terribly worried,' said Andrew. 'I wouldn't be surprised if they're cross with us—at least, until we explain what has happened.'

'Hm, we had better get down quickly, I think,' his brother replied.

Just then, they heard the familiar sound of their mother's voice calling them.

'Tea-time, children. Come on in now. And don't forget to wash your hands.'

'It's Mummy,' gasped Sarah. 'Oh dear! Do you think she's been calling us every day like this? How long have we been away? Perhaps it's sent her mad. Oh, how awful! Mummy! Mummy! We're back. Up here,' she squealed.

Below them moments later, stood the smiling face and red print dress which was mother.

'So there you are,' she laughed. 'I wondered where you'd got to. Have you had a good afternoon?'

The children couldn't believe their ears. Perhaps Sarah was right and she had lost her senses because of their absence.

'Afternoon?' they repeated incredulously.

They quickly slid down the tree and ran into their mother's arms.

'Oh, Mummy, we're so sorry we've been away so long! It's lovely to be back safe and sound. We've had the most marvellous adventure but you must have been terribly worried about us. Have you been very upset?'

Sarah looked up appealingly into her mother's eyes.

'Why, what are you going on about, dear?' her mother said. 'It's only six o'clock. I don't call an afternoon a long time. At least, not long enough to worry about. So what is this marvellous adventure you've had?'

'But we've been away for *days*!' Peter exclaimed, looking puzzled. 'In the Great Forest, fighting the witch and...and....'

He tailed off, for his mother was laughing.

'My, so that's it! You've been making up an adventure. What imaginations!'

'But it's not,' said Andrew. 'It really happened and we were nearly killed. And there was Trotter and Oswain and Arca the eagle and...'

'And lots of others too, if I know you,' his mother interrupted. 'So, where is this Great Forest of yours?'

'It's through that hole in the tree and down the steps inside,' Andrew explained.

'What hole? I can't see one,' she replied.

Together they looked and, sure enough, there was no hole to be seen.

'Well...well, we've got medals to prove it, anyway,' said Sarah, rather upset. 'Look!'

Mum looked.

'Oh, yes. So I see,' she said unbelievingly, for there was nothing to see.

'Well, feel them then,' challenged Peter. 'Come on, mum.'

'Enough of your games now,' said mother firmly. 'Run along now, all of you. And don't forget to wash those hands! Stairs in the tree indeed! Wait till I tell Father and Uncle Joe.'

'Parents!' declared Andrew emphatically as they walked to the house. 'Why can't they ever believe anything?'

'Children!' mused their mother, smiling to herself.

.   .   *   .   .

That night, three tired children stood at the bedroom window, gazing up into the velvet night sky. Stars hung like jewels in the heavens and they stared silently for a long while.

'Do you think we imagined it all?' asked Andrew.

'No, of course not,' his brother replied. 'I'm sure it happened, even if the grown-ups don't believe us.'

'What do you think, Sarah?'

Their sister stared quietly at the stars and then spoke slowly.

'I *know* it was all real—and I don't think it's the last time either. I can feel it somehow.'

Her brothers nodded.

Just then, one star seemed to glow more brightly than the rest. They all saw it. And a dark shadow flitted across the sky. Hardly could it be seen, but the sound which followed was unmistakable. A high pitched, eerie screech pierced the gloom and sent shivers down their spines. They clutched at the jewels about their necks and almost felt them.

Unbelievably high in the night sky a great white bird winged his way westwards, and, far below, three pyjama-clad children whispered his name in awe.

'Arca!'

Also by the same author in Kingsway paperback ...

Gublak's Greed

by John Houghton

Powerful forces are on the move...

Princess Alena runs away from home. She has the Star-Pearl with her—

Gublak the goblin wants it more than anything else in the world.

Oswain has a strange dream.

Peter, Sarah and Andrew again find themselves drawn into another realm—

Can they rescue the princess from Gublak's evil clutches?

What is her real identity? Why is the Star-Pearl so important?

Find the answers in this enthralling sequel to HAGBANE'S DOOM.

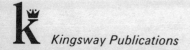
Kingsway Publications

The Healthy Alternative
Which way to wholeness?

by John Houghton

'Crowded city streets full of lonely people . . . hospitals and surgeries jam-packed . . . stress, violence and anxiety like jagged rocks cutting into the souls of millions . . .'

'Gentlemen, is there any cure for this malicious malady? Or shall society merely continue to put its trust in tranquillizers and television to ease this self-inflicted torment? What is to be done . . .?'
That is what I have come to observe,' said the Pilgrim Watcher.

In a unique blend of fictional narrative and stimulating discussion, John Houghton brings together several imaginary characters who offer solutions to the ills of our materialistic Western society.

At the forefront of the story are Mr Aquarius and Mr Christian, both of whom reject the idea that man is just a complex machine. Each champions an alternative way of living, but it soon becomes apparent that they are irreconcilably different from each other. Mr Aquarius seeks to harmonize man and nature through various techniques and diets, while Mr Christian insists that the key to personal wholeness is a life centred on Jesus Christ and worked out in a Spirit-filled community.

As the narrative moves to a breathtaking climax, we are left with a prophetic challenge to seek answers from the source of true wholeness. Either way, we must decide.

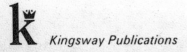

Kingsway Publications